Pretend Plumber
An Adventure

Stephanie Barbé Hammer

AN INLANDIA INSTITUTE PUBLICATION

INLANDIA
INSTITUTE

RIVERSIDE, CALIFORNIA

Permissions
Inlandia Institute
4178 Chestnut Street
Riverside CA 92501

Book layout & design: Mark Givens
Cover photograph by Bil Gaines
Printed and bound in the United States
Distributed by Ingram

Library of Congress Cataloging-in-Publication Data

Names: Hammer, Stephanie Barbé, author.
Title: Pretend plumber : an adventure / Stephanie Barbé Hammer.
Description: Riverside, California : Inlandia Institute, [2022] | Summary:
    Sarassine Anfang, a precocious Los Angeles teen, is so fed up with her
    dysfunctional Jewish Hancock Park family that she decides to run away to
    her grandfather's Wilshire condo and become a plumber, but her
    chocolate-eating grandmother and her distracted parents have other
    ideas.
Identifiers: LCCN 2022011568 (print) | LCCN 2022011569 (ebook) | ISBN
    9781955969048 (paperback) | ISBN 9781955969116 (ebook)
Subjects: CYAC: Identity--Fiction. | Family life--Fiction. | Jews--Fiction.
    | Grandparents--Fiction. | Runaways--Fiction. | Plumbers--Fiction.
Classification: LCC PZ7.1.H36326 Pr 2022 (print) | LCC PZ7.1.H36326
    (ebook) | DDC [Fic]--dc23
LC record available at https://lccn.loc.gov/2022011568
LC ebook record available at https://lccn.loc.gov/2022011569

Published by Inlandia Institute
Riverside, California
www.InlandiaInstitute.org
First Edition

Pretend Plumber

STEPHANIE BARBÉ HAMMER

For Paula —

[signature]

august 2022

For Janet, who suggested I write a pretend novel

and

For Andrea, who knows everything about Los Angeles

"For although I feel that I know a tremendous lot, I am not yet aware how much there is in the world to find out about. It will take me a little time to discover whether I am very wise or very foolish."

— L. Frank Baum, *The Marvelous Land of Oz*

Contents

CHAPTER 1

The trouble below starts with the floor. Tomy and Sofia are cleaning our small but location-perfect Hancock Park, Los Angeles house when Tomy notices that a marble floor tile has come loose. He always notices stuff, Tomy does. He should have been an architect or a contractor or a subcontractor but instead he has this job with Sofia cleaning rich people's houses, although we aren't rich.

But it's true: my mom and dad have enough money to hire a husband and wife team to come in twice a week, and we have a cook some days.

So yeah, I guess we're pretty rich, if you think about it. I mean, relatively speaking.

But Tomy says to me—because I am the only one home, and Olia is cooking and can't speak English, so it comes down to me, because I'm not a maniac like my mother and father. A bit of an unfair designation but what do you expect from an overly educated, mature, only-child adolescent?

Yes, I know I'm about to graduate from eighth grade and I've had my bat mitzvah and I'm turning fourteen in July, and *mazel tov you are a woman*. But still really I'm just a KID, for God's sake—so, give me a break. And anyway, the floor.

What was I going to say Tomy was going to say?

Right. Here it is.

Tomy says, "Sarassine (I know, I have a weird French name), do you see that the floor tile is loose?"

"No," I say, and then I say, "Yeah, maybe I noticed."

Also, I have something called *dyspraxia*. Which means I am physically uncoordinated, have issues with organization, and I have short-term memory problems. AKA, I don't remember things sometimes.

But I *did* notice something was wrong with the floor. When I was watching *Pan's Labyrinth* with Charlus (I know, his name is weirdly French too), he got up and then I got up also, because I had to remind him not to use my bathroom, but to use my parents' because I don't like anyone using my bathroom (long story). When I stood and walked away from the Pottery Barn sofa that we got because it's casual and the sofa cover can be machine washed, I felt one of the floor tiles wriggle, making a tipping sound—not a creak, but rather a groan, and slide-y whoosh that a concrete door makes in order to reveal a secret lair that Dr. No has in one of those old James Bond movies.

"Is this important?" I say to Tomy, which sounds rude, but it isn't because one of the things I've learned from my therapist Dr. Gregorian is that I have to signal to people that they need to be really clear if they want me to remember something. One way to do that is to say, "Is this important?" with the implication being "Why? Please explain." Which Tomy does.

"It means there is something wrong below," he says to me.

Something IS wrong, I almost tell him. *Below the surface there is A LOT wrong.*

But instead I say, "What do you mean?"

"The pipes," he says.

"Oh," I say. "That's for my mom and dad to deal with."

"But your parents aren't home right now, Sarassine," says Tomy. "So, you'll need to tell them what I said. Will you remember?"

"Of course I will," I say. Which means I probably won't, because this information does not sound very important ultimately, and that means that I'll probably file it away in the forget-me-zone of neurodivergence, which a lot of famous people now claim to have so that they can have an excuse for being disorganized and "creative."

Dr. Gregorian—who lives in Santa Monica, and who used to be a philosophy professor but decided that the university was boring, so he went back to med school and became a doctor even though he is old—tells me that dyspraxia makes life hard for me sometimes. But he repeatedly tells me: I'm still super-valuable (even though testing reveals that I'm only of average intelligence) because I have genuine empathy. I'll add that I also have a talent for languages, a love of acting, and what someone on the original circa late 1950s *Perry Mason* calls "the gift of the gab."

Also, I'm super-tall, and that's handy for reaching high shelves. And, I have a super-fast metabolism, so I can eat and eat. Which is lucky because I'm always hungry.

Although, come to think of it, I do remember some things, like I just remembered all that information I said just now.

I'm about to sit back down and start up the movie, when I realize that Charlus has been in the bathroom quite a long time. So, I go and knock on the door. And I ask a classic question, which is "What happened—did you FALL IN?"

I don't know why but saying that very old joke always makes me laugh and it usually makes Charlus laugh. But, this time there is silence. I bang on the door again and repeat my all-the-time-getting-less-droll question, until finally, Charlus's voice says, "I think you better look at this."

I'm not sure I like that suggestion coming from someone who's been sitting on the toilet for fifteen minutes. But we ARE friends, deep friends, adopted sibling friends, because we've known each other since elementary school, and we both like to pretend and dress up and act things out, and Charlus can really play guitar and sing.

So, I say "OK," and I turn the gold handle of our bathroom door, and I walk in.

Good news: Charlus has his pants on and isn't sitting on or kneeling in front of the toilet. He's standing there and pointing to the bathtub.

Bad news: the tub is filled with dirty water. Sort of green brown.

"Jesus," I say.

He says, "It's just there, bubbling up from below."

Add to that a smell like rotten eggs and peeling paint and garbage and well—not surprisingly—a bit like shit.

Tomy comes in.

"That's what I'm talking about," he says. "You need to call your parents."

I don't want to call them.

Dad is very busy practicing law, and in his spare time studying Torah and the *New Testament* with famous professors at the Hebrew Unified University of American Rabbis Here To Make the World Better and Not Worse which is in Santa Monica and hard to get to using mass transit (but if you bring your car you'll never find parking, because Santa Monica), while Mom is equally busy helping to run an art gallery that focuses uniquely on collages right near the Goethe Institute in the Miracle Mile, and as a result she lives almost exclusively in an abstract world of ideas while

---

✡ **Torah Technicalities**

IMHO, "The Torah" generally refers to like the most important part of the Hebrew Bible which is the first five books of Moses which are *Genesis, Exodus, Leviticus, Numbers,* and *Deuteronomy* OR if you want to be fancy and Jewish-accurate, *Bereshit, Shemot, Vayikra, Bemidbar*, and *Devarim*. But Torah can also refer to the whole Hebrew Bible (which has got the Prophets in it and the Psalms and Judges and junk like that), AND there's also a difference between oral Torah and written Torah, although I don't get that part exactly. Oh! And it's written in Hebrew and it's also written on a big scroll although of course there are regular book versions. A book with pages like we're used to is called a **codex**. My dad taught me that.

speaking German because most of the collagists are German. This means she tends to go hide in her office at the gallery when you tell her there's a problem. Also, as she's from Manhattan and grew up in apartments, she, to quote her, "doesn't know from houses."

I love Mom and Dad but these days I don't like them much. I mean, stop talking about the Bible and papier mâché and deal with the pipes why don't you? And also, why aren't you guys ever home, when Dad, your office is in Century City, and Mom, your office is just down on Wilshire, and you don't even work full-time? I mean, I'm just asking.

It's weird how your feelings about people change.

Like when Charlus told me last week that he had a feeling that he was really a girl, despite the fact that he has a penis, and looks like a boy; he says his therapist says that lots of people make that decision to "change their gender assignment."

Can you even do that?

Apparently, the answer is yes.

Actually my feelings about Charlus *did* change, BUT they changed for the better because I was so impressed by a fifteen-year-old person who says *I'm a girl*, and who insists to themselves and the world *I don't care what's down below.*

What is below may or may not matter.

But in our immediate case, it *matters*. If the plumbing doesn't work you can't take a dump, and you can't take a shower, and you can't wash the dishes, and you can't do the laundry. And things smell, and things back up.

This happens to us a lot. The plumbing in our house is bad, because our pipes are old. So the pipes leak stuff. We all know this.

There are advantages to this um, seepage. Our next-door neighbors who run an unlicensed daycare center complain that our roses are flourishing in our backyard while their lemons are dying, and they want to know our secret for making this weird desert ground that we have in LA actually grow something.

"What fertilizer are you using and why are you such selfish people that you won't share?" the neighbor asked my mother one day.

"Because the fertilizer we are using is our own shit," my mother told her in a somewhat snippy voice because she had just had an emergency in the autobiographical 3D collage exhibit with an artist from Vienna and she was more than a little cranky.

"FINE," said the neighbor. "Don't tell us."

"OK," I say to Tomy. "I'll make a call."

CHAPTER 2

I call my mother first, but the call goes straight to voicemail.

"*Ihr Ruf ist sehr wichtig,*" the greeting says.

I try texting. No response.

Then I call my father, but my GPS reveals that he's with my mother. They are doing something at the Hancock Park City Hall Annex. They are perhaps talking to an attorney or a judge because they are getting a divorce.

They were separated for a year. They are back together, but they each go to their own therapist as well as to couples therapy. AND each one of them goes on these surprise "trips" for their mental health.

Charlus thinks it's suspicious too.

The question now is who to call.

I think about calling Ryan the depressive contractor who says he can fix anything and do anything, but you have to call him very early in the morning, which I am not doing, but then Charlus yells from the bathroom, "There's more water coming up through the drain!"

"Sarassine, you need to call a plumber yourself," Tomy says. He is dusting with a Swiffer and trying not to look like he's eavesdropping, but I'll tell you anyone lurking with a Swiffer in hand looks highly suspect, to once again quote the original *Perry Mason*.

"I don't know any plumbers and I have homework," I say. Charlus comes back to the couch, waiting to resume the movie, but even he rolls his eyes a bit at that one, because the fact is we are almost on summer vacation from eighth grade, and all we really have left to do is prepare for our class play.

Tomy suggests looking online or even finding an old *Yellow Pages*, because we have kept all of the phone books since we moved here.

"HARD COPIES," my mother tells me at least four times a week. "We might have an apocalyptic internet collapse and we'll need HARD COPIES."

"But then the phones won't work either," I say.

"Then, we'll burn the books for warmth in the fireplace like they do in *The Day After Tomorrow*, Sarassine," my mom answers.

Sometimes I remind my mom that in SoCal keeping warm is not an issue.

Lately, I just go "uh-huh," and go watch some of *The Day After Tomorrow*, which is actually pretty good.

But today, I bypass all that and call the one person I know will come.

And that's Mr. Pasternak.

Mr. Pasternak is my grandfather's handyman and he's crazy and my father hates him, but he *does* answer the phone right away.

"Just a SECOND," he yells. He does a lot of yelling, because he is Israeli, and he also has false teeth, which he dropped off the balcony of my grandfather's Wilshire condo one time when he was yelling. The teeth hit an ex-football player on the head as he was getting into his Hummer, but my grandfather talked the football player out of suing, because he's charming like that.

My grandfather, Hans Anfang, is—with my mother's encouragement—writing a speculative fiction novel based on his life as a kid in Germany before he escaped Hitler and became a 4-H Club apprentice produce farmer in San Diego. I say, "The book sounds scary" and he says "It's fine because nothing bad ever happens in the book"—which I find hard to imagine since Nazi Germany is involved. But he says, "It's utopian speculative fiction, which means Hitler never comes to power because Rosa Luxemburg becomes prime minister, so it's about as politically progressive as you can get." He's hoping to get the local chapter of the Green Party to let him back in after the leadership expelled him for repeatedly yelling at everyone to arrive on time.

Germans are into punctuality.

At this point Mr. Pasternak interrupts my train of thought and says, "Miss Sarassine, where your folks?"

I'm sorry to do this chopped up talking in English, but he really DOES talk like that, and I'm trying to give you a sense of the characters, which is what my grandfather says makes really powerful storytelling.

Charlus and I continue watching *Pan's Labyrinth* while we wait for Mr. Pasternak to come over. Charlus insisted that I watch the movie, but I find it extremely scary. It is bright sunshine out, but the TV screen makes me look over my shoulder at the wall in back of me every five minutes.

"What the hell are you doing?" Charlus asks. "Do you have a nervous tick? Am I going to have to try to explain you to strangers on the street and say, 'This is my demented friend who can't control her bodily movements'?"

"Very funny," I say.

But the fact is the movie is making me think about darkness, although it is bright sunshine and June and hot in Hancock Park, and somehow the sludge in the tub makes me think of darkness too, and yes, I know I'm too old to have such fears, for God's sake, but I have them anyway. I just don't tell anyone the fact that maybe, just maybe I see spirits sometimes. Well I don't see them. I feel like I'm *about* to see them.

Dr. Gregorian thinks this is early childhood trauma of some sort.

But Charlus and his whole family think that spirits are real.

Charlus interrupts my train of thought, "You're not watching the movie!"

I shrug.

"OK," he says, grabbing the remote and doing some very fast clicking and scrolling. "How about this?"

And there we are looking at a woman masturbating in a tub in her bathroom.

"*The Shape of Water*," he says. "Same director and same actor!"

The woman masturbating in the tub is freaking me out, although I have to tell you, it's a great looking bathroom! Big rectangular tiles on the wall, and those cool little octagon tiles on the floor! And a nice big tub.

But I don't want to watch anyone masturbate, so I move my eyes down to the floor and that's when I notice that Charlus is wearing my bright red bat mitzvah Gucci sling-backs. They are too small for him, and his heels hang over the back, which my mother says is a sure sign that your shoes don't fit and is also kind of trashy looking. But I actually like them on him.

"Do you want to keep those?" I say.

He says, "Maybe."

I say, "You stretched them out anyway so you might as well take them."

He says, "OK."

The doorbell rings.

Great! It's Mr. Pasternak.

What? You've never been to a bar mitzvah? The least you need to know:

A **"bar mitzvah"** is a Jewish religious service indicating that the person in question—a young person of thirteen—is now "bar mitzvah" which means son of the mitzvot, which is plural for mitzvah which is what non-Jews call "commandments." Only, we don't have just ten, we have 613, which is a lot. Anyhow, if you're a girl, you have a bat mitzvah which means daughter of the mitzvot, and if you're gender nonbinary I'm not sure what you do, but it's an interesting question (update: a friend of a friend just told me that for nonbinary folx, you use the plural b'nai mitzvah [just like using the plural in English! {which makes total sense}]). This religious service is held on a Saturday, and the bar/bat mitzvah generally reads a section from the Torah out loud in Hebrew in a kind of sing-songy voice and then they give a little speech in English (or in whatever the language is of the congregation) about what that section of the Torah means to them, and there's a big bunch of food to eat afterwards and sometimes there's a party at night where there's another big bunch of food, because Judaism and food, duh. Protip: If you're going to a bar/bat mitzvah find out if it's Reform, Reconstructionist, Conservative or Orthodox, because the dress code differs, because Judaism is complicated. Also bring a gift, or money in an envelope for the bar/bat mitzvah. Gifts accepted until the bar/bat/bnai mitzvah is eighteen. Just kidding (not really).

CHAPTER 3

Mr. Pasternak comes in with two guys who speak only Russian and two guys who speak something else, but it isn't Ukrainian, because Tomy shakes his head at them, and then he and Sofia look at each other, shrug their shoulders, and start stripping the beds.

Charlus wants to watch some more of *The Shape of Water*, but the men are examining the tippy marble tiles in the family room/ den, and my room is too messy to watch a movie in, and Tomy and Sofia are in my parents' room, so that just leaves the living room, and there's no TV in there and who wants to watch a movie on a computer if you don't have to?

So, we give up on that activity and use the living room as a performance space to practice our parts for the production of *Twelfth Night,* which our English class is putting on for End of the Year Parents' Visitation of the Children in Their Glory Day.

Charlus and I are both disappointed in our parts. I'm playing Sir Toby Belch, when I wanted to play that depressed Count Orsino guy, and Charlus is playing Sir Andrew Aguecheek which he's very bummed out about because he wanted to play a girl—Viola of course, because she is the hero, or Olivia because she's pretty, or even the smart-ass maid girl because she's sexy and fun.

But Ms. Victory said he couldn't, even after he pointed out that either part would do for him, because "Olivia" and "Viola" were almost anagrams of each other, which I thought was a pretty brilliant observation.

"I don't see WHY," says Charlus to me. "I mean all the women's parts were played by boys in Shakespeare, and since I identify more as a girl, I'm perfect."

"I don't know what to do with this line of argumentation, as they say on the PBS *News Hour*," I say. "Let's just figure out how to make Sir Toby and Sir Andrew as funny as possible so we steal the show."

"Good plan!" says Charlus, and we start working on his entrance.

SIR ANDREW

Sir Toby Belch! How now, Sir Toby Belch!

SIR TOBY BELCH

Sweet Sir Andrew!

We think we should do a big bromance kind of hug thing, but just as we are going to swoop and hug and pound each other on the back, Mr. Pasternak's Russian guys and the other guys speaking a different foreign language run right between us, and out the front door and leave the door open, and the flies come in. Then, just as we have shut the door and are getting ready to try again, they come back in with a bunch of machinery, while Mr. Pasternak informs me that he will "go out and look under house." After the machinery goes through the living room, Mr. P comes back through and is talking on the phone very loudly in what I presume is Hebrew because he says "*Ken Ken*" all the time, which I explain to Charlus is not a person named Ken, but rather "yes."

Next, we hear a loud drilling sound, so I give up trying to learn lines such as "Some are born great, some achieve greatness, and some something." Then, unfortunately a helicopter starts flying overhead very low and Charlus freaks out and goes and hides under our very nice Design Within Reach chaise lounge because his family on his father's side is from Haiti, and he says that his dad still worries that the *Tonton Macoute* people might come after him.

His mother is from Missouri and is very blonde, and white. So Charlus is kind of like the former president, I tell him.

"It's very cool to be biracial," I say.

"Spoken like a white person," he says from his place under the sofa.

We try to wait out the drilling. But we get bored with *Twelfth Night,* so we microwave some popcorn in the kitchen, and we decide we want to at least try to at last finish watching *The Shape of Water,* which Charlus assures me will get better and has an even better sex in the bathroom scene that I will really love and that it only gets really violent at the end.

But what I said about the plan going to hell is doubly true when we see what's happening in the erstwhile family room, as they say on KCRW when that man with the nasal voice starts talking about important books in the afternoon.

"Wow," says Charlus, "*c'est vraiment le bordel.*" Charlus lapses into French when he's trying to impress strangers OR when he is really and truly surprised by something.

Mr. Pasternak and his associates have torn up the den room floor and put yellow police tape around it and they have started building things called "cripple walls" even though the pipe problem has not been fixed yet, and the water in the tub that Charlus saw—it seems like years ago now—is still sort of gurgling there even as Mr. Pasternak is telling me the following:

"I get guy to come with camera and he take pictures of sewer line pipe in back. We pull up backyard too probably."

Well that's when I decide I've got to get out of here.

This is also when my childhood dream of becoming a plumber gets reborn. My mom's grandfather was a plumber, and he designed the plumbing system for Nordstrom. Now THAT's a system. I heard that story when I was four and promptly started playing a pretend plumber game that I made up where I talked to an evil fairy who had clogged the drains and got rid of her by flushing seven times and singing *"Happy Birthday."*

But my mom isn't handy with tools (she can't cook [she tried to cook an egg in the microwave once {in its shell}]) and neither is my dad. They can't fix anything. So, we're always hiring people. They say dyspraxia runs in families, and I believe it, looking at all of us and our general terribleness at anything athletic and how long it took all of us to learn to tie our shoes.

I survey the damage and conclude that if *I* could learn how to fix things—despite the fact that dyspraxia makes it hard for me to learn things just by watching—I wouldn't need any of these adults running around the house speaking different languages. I could fix the pipes and Charlus and me could get back to practicing and watching our movies.

We retreat to my bedroom.

Charlus is sympathetic to my situation, but the noise gets to him.

"I'm going home," he says. "I'll call my housekeeper to come get me."

"Hey!" I say. "Let's go to my grandpa's condo."

"OK," says Charlus and he gets to work practicing walking in his new sling-backs, while I rustle up the change for the Wilshire bus.

That's one of the great things about Charlus. He's very agreeable.

"I feel quite transformed in these shoes," he says to me.

I put the change in my pocket and study him. He does look a bit different, maybe. Taller of course, but also a bit more slender. Delicate.

"Can you call me something else?" he says.

"Charlene," I say.

"No," he says. "Jackie." He does a very good twirl and stops very close to me.

"And you are my father, because you made me into someone else by giving me your shoes."

"OK, my son, let's call Grandpa."

"Child," Charlus now Jackie says. "And … you need to use different pronouns."

I call my grandfather and tell him we're coming over.

So, we're set to go, and then—the doorbell rings again. I answer, because I figure it's another foreign language person, or maybe the FEDEX delivery person with my *HOW EVERYTHING WORKS ENCYCLOPEDIA.*

But it's not.

It's Grandma standing there in her Zumba™ exercise clothes, and man is she pissed off.

CHAPTER 4

Grandma stomps in and as she stomps, Bobby, the next-door neighbor's cat, tries to sidle in behind her. Bobby decided long ago that we are a much more interesting family than the neighbors, and he comes in on a regular basis when he isn't standing outside looking through the window and meowing at us. Grandma puts her fancy sneaker down hard to stop Bobby, but he skedaddles as someone said once somewhere in a book that I don't quite remember and off he goes into my parents' bedroom. I can hear Sofia yelling "THE CAT THE CAT," while Mr. Pasternak screams, *"KEN KEN,"* and the drilling roars back into action, and my grandma stares at me and at Charlus and says:

"Whaat hahrrible thing are you kids up to now?!"

Grandma is originally from Florida (which she pronounces *Flahrida*), and although she has had speech training like they do in *Pygmalion*—which is a much better movie than that *My Fair Lady* thing with all that huge hair and weird dresses and junk—she still has a Miami accent, particularly when she gets mad.

Charlus, who knows how to deal with very fancy international grandparents who speak French, says, "Good afternoon, Madame Anfang."

"Don't you Madame me," is her response. "I want that you should tell me, Gerry or Louis or whatever your name is what wrahng thing you're doing!"

It's very clear that we haven't done anything wrong, but it's at that point that a guy in a suit, who is talking on his cell phone, trips over my grandmother as he barrels through the door, knocking her down.

"Pardon me Madam," he says as he hoists her to her feet. "I am a part of the plumbing triage assessment team, and we will surveille, recommend and then bring in Mr. Klepner, who is a renowned Beverly Hills Plumber to the stars and whom you may have seen on three episodes of *MY MANSION SUCKS 90210*." He looks at us appraisingly. "Are you perchance involved in the spinoff project, *NOT QUITE RICH ENUFF 90036*?" We gape at him.

"No, that's the family down the street," he says. "Thanks!" He runs off to join the group in the family room that greets him enthusiastically in a variety of lingos.

"Enough already," says Grandma. She grabs me by one arm, and grabs Charlus/Jackie with the other and she hauls us back to the coach house—which is on the other side of the swimming pool—and she sets us to work folding laundry, because we "aren't too good to do an honest day's work."

I wish my parents could come home, but according to my GPS they are still at the City Hall Annex.

"For you I have some plans," she says to me darkly. "I have told your perrents that you should be sent to Jewish Wild Child Wilderness Camp for the summer, and then to a private school."

"I'm already IN a private school," I tell her. I fold socks, by tying them together rather than folding one over the other because that method stretches one out and not the other and weakens the elastic.

"A strictah private school."

I should take a break at this point and tell you that my grandmother is really pretty. She looks much younger than she is because she takes incredible care of her skin with injectables, dermaplaning and microneedling. And she's smart, even though she only went to junior college. She used to be an assistant mystery editor (she worked on a scary book called *Rosemary's Baby*) and she still reads at least two mystery novels a day, and she can talk to you about Agatha Christie 'til the cows come home. My grandfather adored her, despite the fact that she was and is, in her words, *zaftig*—which is Yiddish for "plump"—and is constantly struggling to balance her desire to be thin with her intense love of Godiva "chahklote."

But she got super angry after she got into a freak motorcycle accident when her tai chi instructor gave her a ride to her mahjong club meeting, and we all thought she was going to die.

Of course she didn't die because here she is standing right in front of us supervising a dubious attempt at laundry folding as I'm telling you this story. The point is, she got so mad that people didn't do enough for her, or love her enough, or value her enough, or give her enough presents, or do what she wanted them to do fast enough (like get taken to the newly reopened Getty Mansion on a Friday afternoon by my dad who had a crucial "Torah in Personal Injury Law" seminar that day, so he had to put it off 'til Sunday, which conflicted with her new, injured motorcycle passengers support group meeting), that when she recovered from her multiple injuries, instead of getting happy, and glad, and thankful, and spiritual—the way people get in those movies made for cable—she just got furious. Really furious.

And so if you weren't like her six other genius sons—Dr. Miles Anfang of Miami (renowned plastic surgeon famous for the "Anfang nose"), Chef Jules Anfang (who designs menus for the New York Yankees), Judo medalist Harold Anfang (founder of Jewish Judo Self-Defense Studios in Austin and San Antonio), twin mathematics whizzes Jacob and Esau (who are joint CEOs of the Anfang and Anfang Accounting Firm in Chicago), and the youngest, musical prodigy Zubin Anfang (combination clarinetist and harpist for both Anchorage and Atlanta Philharmonic Orchestras)—well you just didn't count. My father isn't even an entry-level genius; he's just an attorney, who went to UC Davis. And Grandma NEVER liked my mother because my mother wasn't and isn't Jewish, insists on celebrating both Christmas and Easter at our house, and drives a German car.

I think all this and wonder when or if Grandma will notice that Charlus/Jackie is wearing very high-heeled, expensive red Italian sling-back shoes.

But the person Grandma decided that she *really* didn't like was my grandfather, because he made a joke at the hospital about the tai chi instructor thinking he was James Dean because why else would anyone be so *meschugge* (aka crazy) as to drive a motorcycle in LA? So, as soon as she recovered, Grandma threw Grandpa out. Which is why she lives in a huge house in the fanciest part of Pacific Palisades, and he lives in a condo on the Wilshire corridor. They too are getting a divorce.

The assistant to the plumber opens the screen door to the coach house.

"In consultation with our team, I am informing you that WE HAVE SHUT OFF THE WATER," he announces and then slams the door shut.

"YOU BROKE THE PIPES with your make up and your marijuahhna," my grandmother observes.

"What marijuana?" asks Charlus/Jackie. He—oops they—is—I mean are—doing a pretty miserable job folding t-shirts, because they are folding them lengthwise, which makes a crease down the middle (I've been through this before with Grandma).

I try to catch my friend's eye, but they have their head down, trying to not look at Grandma

Grandma doesn't notice at first that Charlus/Jackie is misfolding the t-shirts, because she's too busy making a point with me.

"What about the way you dump brushes into the toilet?" she says to me, wagging her finger with a very large emerald ring on it.

"The brush thing happened once," I remind Grandma, as I continue folding the socks.

Speaking during the laundry punishment is generally risky. But the silence can be even more deadly.

Grandma looks down at the misfolded t-shirts.

"WRAHNG!" she says fiercely, taking the entire pile of shirts and pulling the folds apart. "YOU FOLD THE SLEEVES IN TOWARDS THE CENTAH," she demonstrates. "What's the matter with you? You act like you've never done lahndry in your life."

"I haven't," is the answer.

Charlus I mean Jackie reworks the t-shirts, and they eventually figure out how to tuck the sleeves, and then the sides in and then fold the whole thing in half.

"If not the Wild Child Wilderness camp," she says, "then we'll send you to Jews in Juvie Reform Reform School in Israel."

Charlus I mean Jackie raises their eyebrows. That's the signal for DISTRACT THE GROWNUPS.

"Hey, Grandma," I say. "What about the repairs to the house?" I say. "Don't Mom and Dad need to get a report on what is happening?"

"**Zey shtil!**" she shouts at me, waving her left hand in a huge circle. "I'll call him."

I open my mouth, but no words come out. Charlus I mean Jackie starts coughing. Grandma nods to herself with satisfaction and stomps off again, to the second room in the coach house, which is right through the bathroom. I should be able to hear everything she says, but I can't hear it all be-

 "Zey Shtil" is Yiddish for "Be Silent"

cause the plumber and his assistants have commenced digging up the backyard.

"She's a—. I hate to—, but, as a m—,—a troubled—the best thing is...."

My voice comes back to me.

"Come on, Jackie," I say. "Time to hit the road."

CHAPTER 5

"I'm hungry," ~~Charlus~~ Jackie says, clearing their throat, when we get back into the house and step past the men at work. Olia has gone home, having put the absolutely incredibly tasty chicken Kyiv in the oven. It won't be ready yet, so I start to make sandwiches in the kitchen, because I'm hungry and that's what I always do when I feel sad and a bit stressed out. I make sandwiches and I think about sex.

I get out the bread and the mayo and the mustard and the really good cold cuts from Hancock Deli, and think about *Pan's Labyrinth* and *The Shape of Water*.

I have to tell you something. I think that the guy who plays the faun (and who plays the creature in the *Water* movie)—is sexually attractive. Is it weird that this terrifying film—which is about I guess the Spanish Civil War, which I Googled, and which is the almost the same time as Hitler but not quite Hitler (because as we all know there's nothing like German engineering, I mean look at *Play-mobil*)—is sexual to me? It's a little less weird, maybe, with the water movie with the great

Would it kill you to learn a little history?

The Spanish Civil War was a big deal and had famous authors like George Orwell (whose real name was Eric something) and Ernest Hemingway (boring writer, but still it was good he did this) fighting on the side of a bunch of people who were struggling to prevent a kind of version of the Nazis from taking over the country. This all happened before World War 2, although I guess it kind of overlapped with it, idk tbh. Well, the bad people won and the whole country was run by somebody named Francisco Franco until he died, and then things got better. See https://en.wikipedia.org/wiki/Spanish_Civil_War

......

bathroom—which is clearly all about sex, even though all I saw was like the first ten minutes, which just had the masturbating girl in it.

But still, I wonder.

To be honest, I've haven't had sex with anyone yet, or kissed anyone, even. There's a girl in my class who had sex by accident with her cousin, but how you can have sex by accident loses me completely.

I mean it's probably pretty deliberate, isn't it? I mean, you have to THINK about what you're doing: you take all your clothes off, and you rub bodies, and the guy—or I guess girl, which I think about sometimes too—holds your breasts and then, sticks his or her fingers into your vagina, which certainly feels good as I've tried it on myself and it's definitely a winner as a fun experience, and then you hold the guy's penis, and you put it inside you and he goes in and out with it, and you clench and unclench, and then you have this thing called an orgasm.

I know about this, but tbh, I've never met a real person I want to kiss, or see naked, or any of that stuff. On the other hand, I'm very young, but on the other other hand, Juliet in *Romeo and Juliet* was like my age when she met Romeo and they got married. So I think it depends.

I worry sometimes that I'm behind schedule.

I don't talk about this with anyone, though. Maybe ~~Charlus~~ Jackie would understand, as ~~he~~ they want to have sex or be sexual or kiss or whatever with boys too. But I don't think they are gay. Jackie has something else going on.

CHAPTER 6

I'm thinking very deeply about sex, but I'm also really realizing that if we are going to pretend run away to my grandfather's condo, using mass transit, I had better plan ahead and make more than my usual supply of sandwiches. I take out more cheese, cream cheese, peanut butter, and jelly.

We need water! Because Southern California!

I take out some bottled water, and then I think:

Possible Emergency! So I run back into my bedroom and get a flashlight.

And then I remember that I need to go get my travelers checks that my mom gave me for emergencies when we went to Big Sur by ourselves last year. She said, "You always need money."

And I should get my school I.D. Because you need identification.

I go back into the kitchen, while Jackie practices their part for Sir Andrew.

But guess what? Making sandwiches is a lot of work, and a lot of work is boring, and as you can imagine it's hard for me to concentrate on things for a long time, so I leave all the sandwiches half made and the mayo and the bread and all of it out on the kitchen counter, and I go into the hall to take a break and think of something that I haven't thought of yet but that might come to me if I could keep my brain from whirling around about laundry, and Sir Toby, and Israel, and the faun.

I look down the hall at the front door. Looking into the distance is often refreshing. Perhaps the actual plumber will arrive! Things will get fixed when he does.

Grandma has left her black bag by the front door. It's a big expensive bag. If the witches in *Macbeth* were rich, Jewish, and living in Pacific Palisades, they'd have a bag like that.

I go over to the front door. Jackie has given up practicing their lines (it IS a very small part) and is lounging on the super modern but not very comfortable Italian sofas. But they perk up when they see me looking at the bag.

"What all is in there?" they say. They walk over and grab one of the floppy handles.

"Don't take anything," I say but they're already pulling stuff out of it. Handkerchiefs, mostly. Crumpled up.

"Why do ALL grandmothers have these cloth things?" they ask rhetorically, waving them around as lint scatters.

More stuff comes out. Lipsticks, Motrin bottles, receipts, and then....

A big yellow book with a cartoon of a clueless-looking guy holding his hands up.

"Those graphics look familiar," says Jackie.

"It looks like a *For Dummies* book," I say, "my mom loves these." It's true. We got a million of them scattered around the house.

"But what language is the title in?" Jackie says.

It's Hebrew. And the letters read:

קבלה מעשית למטומטמים

But underneath is the translation:

Practical Kabbalah for Total Schlubs

What's a "schlub"?

This is another Yiddish word, and it means a dumb person or a blockhead, or a noodlehead or a peabrain, nitwit, numbskull—you get the idea.

Jackie grabs the book.

"Look at the back!":

> Note: Contents to be used only as appropriate by a licensed practitioner. Failure to comply may cause extreme reactions.
>
> Questions? call 1818.
>
> Product of the Kishef Center in collaboration with the ZAUBER International Project

"What's Kishef?" Jackie asks.

I take my phone out of my pocket and find out that **Kishef** means *magic*.

"Ah!" exclaims Jackie. "*Enfin* your *grand-mère* has turned out to be INTERESTING—she's a witch after all!"

I sigh.

"I doubt it. If that's the case, why doesn't she just fix the plumbing?"

"*Les sorcières.... elles ne font pas des choses comme ça—*"

"English!"

"Witches don't do things like that, mundane things. They fly and turn you into a statue and they have a cat!"

"I don't think Jews are supposed to do that kind of stuff."

"Wait—" says Jackie. "Isn't kabbalah that thing that that white rock 'n' roll Vogue lady is into?"

"You mean Madonna?"

"Yeah—So what IS it?"

I Google "Practical Kabbalah" and get a bunch of incredibly long articles, but I share my screen with Jackie and we kind of figure out:

- Practical kabbalah is a type of Jewish mysticism that deals with the use of magic.

- Apparently certain kinds of magic are OK to practice but only a special elite group of people are allowed to do magic, and even this special elite group is only permitted to do magic under certain circumstances, and we can't figure out what those circumstances are exactly.

- There are spells, I guess you'd call them, having to do with angelic names, using the divine (whatever that is) and using amulets and incantations.

- Then there's this other "kabbalah" that's more thinky and involves trying to understand things like the nature of God and the nature of existence through study (of course ... it's always studying with Judaism, isn't it?) and meditation.

- These days (and since almost always) this magical type of kabbalah seems to be frowned upon, as my mom would say, which means it's forbidden-ish and you're not supposed to do it, but some people still do it anyway, it seems like.

"Ugh," says Jackie. "Meditation."

"I think we should take the book," I say, as I grab *Practical Kabbalah for Total Schlubs* from Jackie.

"Be careful—it's really heavy."

"No, it isn't," I say. "It's super light—what's the matter with you? I'll just stick it in my backpack."

"But won't she notice if it's gone?" says Jackie.

I look at the bookshelves in the living room and grab the first *For Dummies* book I see.

"I'll just substitute the one book for the other!"

"Genius!" says Jackie as I take the *Practical Kabbalah for Total Schlubs* book and put it on the counter next to the sandwiches. I make a few more sandwiches and put some of the stuff away in the fridge, while Jackie continues practicing their sexy walk. Then I organize the supplies.

I am packing up all the sandwiches, and the change for the bus, and my travelers checks, and the water, and some brownies, and some tissues, and some Motrin, and my extra pair of glasses, and some gum, and my dyspraxia meds, and my retainer, and my smart phone, and my charger (it's hard travelling light in the Twenty-First Century, I can tell you), and the book.

Jackie follows me from room to room, teetering on their heels. "This will be an exciting adventure because you are not just my friend, but my father. You have created me in my new feminine form and so I will go wherever you lead me."

I chuckle. "I'm not your father!"

"But you are!" they say. They reach up, putting their hands on my shoulders. I am much taller than them, even in heels, so I do feel a bit parental. They stand on tiptoe and bring their face close to mine.

"You are giving me hope," they say in a quiet voice, "that one day I can have surgery so that my outside can fit my insides. And.... I can run away for real if I have to."

I put my hands on Jackie's hands. Jackie's hands are broad and substantial, but they are trembling. And they feel sweaty on my shoulders.

I inhale and exhale. My therapist Dr. Gregorian says that's always a good thing to do when you feel a rush of anxiety or worry.

Then I think of something.

"If you are going to trend towards Jackie then you need a different outfit to go with those shoes." My friend who used to be Charlus and who now identifies as Jackie is wearing baggy shorts and a vintage VELVET GOLDMINE t-shirt and that sure won't work.

So, we try a few outfits in my closet, but my friend formerly known as Charlus and who now identifies as Jackie doesn't look good in any of my outfits—Jackie is a little petite for the tall size I wear. So we go into my parents' bedroom.

Please note how my pronoun change is working. It takes some getting used to, but it's totally doable. You just have to focus.

......

We walk into my mom's closet.

"I'm not ready for a skirt," Jackie warns. "So, I need an interim look."

Accordingly, we pick out a great leather jacket and some stretch pants.

"Nice," they say. "Patti Smith." We take one of my father's white shirts and add a long black tie. It hangs down long so it looks a little like a dress but isn't, quite.

I stick Jackie's "Charlus" shorts and shirt into my backpack along with their Converses, so they don't get left behind in the mess of cripple walls and multilingual yelling.

"Let's go," I say. We walk out towards the front door.

Then Grandma comes back in.

"I'm going to move in here," she announces. "Your perrents aren't coming home, and they say I can use their room. Tomahrrow we'll drive you up to Jewish Wild Child Wilderness Camp."

I roll my eyes. Grandma and her grand plans.

Jackie says, "Don't tell me you're having your house redone as well?"

"Tented," says Grandma. "Termites." She looks at my friend's new outfit.

"And you're supposed to be who? Buddy Hahlly?"

I decide to just answer, "Yes."

We wait for Grandma to go back to the backyard and settle in and practice her Jewish magic or do whatever it is she is doing by herself all the time in that huge house that she lives in all alone without Grandpa. So, Jackie and I sit on the front steps of the house for a while, and we eat a couple of the sandwiches and watch an old guy yell at a young guy driving a stretch limousine up and down our street, pulling into driveways and then backing out of them.

"NO," yells the older man. "You gotta pull in with an elegant swoop and not slam on the brakes."

The driver doesn't answer.

"ARE YOU DEAF?" says the older man.

I feel bad for the young guy trying to learn to drive a limo.

I feel bad for Sofia and Tomy who have to work so hard all the time.

I feel bad for Mr. Pasternak and his false teeth.

I start to feel bad for myself and I think about Dr. Gregorian saying when you start to feel badly you need an action plan, because the worst thing to feel is to feel powerless.

I like that idea. If there's trouble below, you can't just stand still and wait for the tubes to explode with gunk, and goo, and hair, and brushes, and whatever got flushed down by accident. You've got to get out of there and get some perspective and get help from your grandfather who survived the Holocaust because some German lady pretended to BE a plumber, walked into his house in Frankfurt, and walked out with him hidden inside her tool kit.

CHAPTER 7

Google search results:

> Plumbing school = no results
>
> Plumbing capital = Kansas City Plumbing Fixtures—we're One Hundred Years old!
>
> Plumbing experts = do you mean plumming experts?
>
> Jewish plumbers = invalid search

Sponsored: Tired of paying exorbitant bills?

> Had it with sanitation systems that don't measure up?
>
> Call or email us for a free estimate.
>
> Flushing Plumbing contractors in Flushing, NY
>
> WE TRAVEL EVERYWHERE THROUGH OUR SPECIAL TUBES
>
> *Times* Review headline: This Nimble Island Shakespeare Festival Production of *Twelfth Night* Plumbs What Identity Can Mean.

Related:

> Plumb the depths. At a price you can afford. Is your blockage physical or spiritual? Email: delve567@aol.com

CHAPTER 8

Grandma ought to come and get us to come in from sitting on the uncomfortable steps and then give us a yummy dinner, but my mom once told me that Grandma had issues with social anxiety so that when Dad was growing up, on her days off from mystery editing, she would hide herself in the garage, and alternate eating Godiva chocolates with intensive sit-ups and jumping jacks while watching Jack LaLanne and later Jane Fonda exercise shows on a portable TV.

That's what she does now. Grandma grabs a huge chocolate box from her giant bag, yells at us that she isn't going to bother to make us dinner because, according to her, we've ruined our appetites with all those "hahrrible sandwiches," tells Jackie to go home and announces that she needs privacy and is going to practice tai chi. This means that she will go into my parents' room, and shut the door, and eat candy (even though she isn't supposed to consume any sweets post-motorcycle accident), and learn her latest Zumba routine. Then speed read another mystery.

Sofia and Tomy leave. The workmen leave. The plumber's assistant leaves.

The last one out is Mr. Pasternak.

"They all come back tomorrow, Miss Sarassine," he says.

And then he says. "It's time for me to leave you."

"What do you mean?" I say.

He lights a cigarette, and he offers me one. And because I'm a teenager and you have to take what you can get, I take the cigarette and he lights it with his lighter.

"It's time to go home."

"Home where?" I ask after I finish my novice smoker coughing which they always do in the movies because it actually is what you do when you smoke a cigarette for the first time.

"Jaffa," he says. I look back at him with a blank expression and he says, "Israel."

"Wait," I say. "you mean—"

"Jaffa is hometown," he says. "I come back in month, probably"

He walks off. Why is everyone obsessed with a place that is the size of New Jersey and that has people shooting at each other all the time?

I'd ponder that problem, but I have—as they say—other fish to fry.

Is Hancock Park my *hometown*? I can't think of a place that feels less like that than this.

The streetlights come on, although it's still light out.

We live near the biggest Orthodox shul—that's synagogue—west of the Mississippi, and there are men in black hats, and women in wigs, and lots of kids in and out of strollers, walking up the street, because it's about to be *Shabbat*, and if you're religious—which we aren't—you go and sit in services for a really long time and then you come home and you eat a huge meal.

 "Shabbat" is Hebrew for

"Sabbath" which runs from Friday night to Saturday night for Jews and if you're very religious you don't write, use money, work, turn on lights, or drive a car which is why all these Orthodox Jews are walking on the sidewalk in LA, which as you know is unusual because to quote that song that my parents like, "Nobody Walks in LA," although we do, because we're kids.

Jackie and I stand up and watch the men in black hats walk by our house. The adults don't look at us, because we aren't "observant Jews," but two little girls and one boy turn around, and wave shyly at me and at Jackie.

We start walking too. We pass the limo guy trying and failing to swoop up the driveway with the requisite elegance, as they say on *Project Runway* or *America's Next Top Model.*

 Just in case you've been speaking to some Holocaust deniers or Neo-Nazis,

the Holocaust (which Jews also call the "Shoah" which means "catastrophe" I think) was a real thing that happened that was terrible, and my rabbi said that the Jews are still down 4 million people, which means the genocide was so successful we're still building back up our population and may never do it. Of course genocide isn't original. We learned about this in school. The Trail of Tears, and Wounded Knee, and the enslavement of African people—all of that happened here in the US, much earlier and the Armenian genocide came before the Holocaust too. I have always wondered why our genocide kind of put genocide on the map as a thing to condemn and fight against. But my Torah tutor got very uncomfortable, when I asked the question: "why does our genocide get so much attention?"

Anyway, just to be clear

The Holocaust really happened. 6 million Jews died. It happened in Europe between 1941 and 1945. See

https://en.wikipedia.org/wiki/The_Holocaust See also Bloxham, Donald. The Final Solution: A Genocide. Oxford: Oxford University Press. 2009 ISBN 978-0-19-955034-0 and "Killing Centers: An Overview," Holocaust Encyclopedia, United States Holocaust Memorial Museum, https://web.archive.org/web/20170914220116/ and https://www.ushmm.org/wlc/en/article.php?ModuleId=10005145

"Wasn't your grandfather in the Holocaust?" Jackie asks me.

"Almost," I say. "A pretend plumber saved him."

We find the bus stop for the RAPID which is in my opinion the best bus in town. There's a man who works at Rite Aid waiting at the stop along with two old ladies.

"How?" asks Jackie right before they (and by "they" I mean Jackie and not the little old ladies) fall in a heap on the pavement.

"I've broken the heel of my shoe," they announce, still lying down.

"She hid him," I say, pulling them to their feet. I'm about to get to the special toolbox detail that the pretend plumber used to save Jewish children when a black limo comes careening around the corner and comes to a screeching halt at the bus stop, which I'm pretty sure is illegal but I'm sure not one to issue a citizen's arrest— whatever that is.

"I'm not taking any more crap from you!" yells the limo driver, as the older guy on the passenger side gets out.

"You'll never make it as a chauffeur in this town," yells the man who gets out.

"The hell with you and your lousy, unhelpful coaching," says the driver. "It's my uncle's car, and I'll get him to sign my limousine paperwork as soon as he gets back into the country."

The teacher/instructor walks off in a huff, as they say, and then the driver rolls the window down and says, "Hey—do you kids need a ride?"

My mom says to never get in a car with someone you don't know, so I just say something polite but nondescript that I heard someone say on the original *Perry Mason*, which I should have mentioned before, my father watches all the time, even though he knows all the plot points backwards and forwards.

I say, "Listen Mister, we don't want any trouble," which sounds pretty cool I have to admit, although as I look at the face of the chauffeur student, I realize that the chauffeur is actually a very pretty girl.

"Oh my God," says the driver to Jackie, "I love your shoes!"

My dad started watching reruns of the 1950s *Perry Mason* TV show in law school and he never stopped. He watches the shows over and over. "The shows are so comforting," he always tells me. "The mystery is always discovered, and the matter is always straightened out."

CHAPTER 9

Jackie opens the rear door to the limousine.

"You can't get in," I say.

"But dear Father," Jackie says. "I can't go any further with my shoes."

The girl chauffeur—she looks so young with the inside car lights turned on—nods thoughtfully with her cap on, and I notice she has like short shorts on and stockings and nice shoes herself.

She says to me, "OK, you're right not to be so trusting. Also, to be honest, I'm not exactly quite a legal chauffeur yet."

Jackie smiles apologetically on behalf of my paranoid response to the lovely driver.

The not quite a chauffeur tips her hat.

"But someday soon," she says. "I'll have my official permit and I'll give you a ride for free."

She reaches across and hands me something through the open window.

I lean through and take her card.

Mariama Mbabe —
apprentice chauffeur

"Thanks," I say.

Mariama drives away. I put the card in my jeans pocket, while Jackie sighs and puts on their Converses, which I brought along, because I am pretty WELL ORGANIZED despite the dyspraxia.

The bus comes. We get on and we sit.

The bus is crowded. There are nurses going to work at the UCLA hospital, and high-school kids a little older than us, and people LOTS older than us speaking in languages that are so different and so cool sounding we think we're at the UN and not in our plain old weird American city. Jackie puts their head on my shoulder.

"I'm tired," they say.

I am too but we've just started and I'm Jackie's parent, so I have to act energetic the way my mom used to act when I was trying and failing to learn either dance routines or tennis at school. That was before my diagnosis.

"Let's practice our lines," I say.

We talk about being up betimes, and we talk about Malvolio's stockings, and we talk about the tricks we are going to play on him and how funny the party after the show is going to be. How everyone is going to say, "You guys were amazing, you totes stole the show!"

I realize I sort of like Sir Toby.

Some men are born great, some achieve greatness, and some—

How does the rest go?

Westwood looks a little like the movie *Metropolis*—the old silent movie that Jackie says influenced the voguing rock and roll lady (**Madonna,** I remind him) and a lot of other pop stars. It's all fancy apartment buildings where everything is marble and light. I feel like I'm entering a new kingdom. We cross the street and walk past the church stuck right there between the high buildings, and we go into Grandpa's building.

"I'm Mr. Anfang's granddaughter," I tell the doorman. The assistant doorman looks for a car and is shocked that we have apparently arrived here on foot.

"And?" says the doorman looking at Jackie.

"A friend," I say.

And we get shown to the elevator that opens on both sides depending on where you are going because if you live in this building you get half a floor. The apartments are that big.

I feel excitement and relief and confidence. My grandfather is my father's father and he's going to make it all right.

CHAPTER 10

When the elevator door opens, my grandfather is standing in the hallway in front of the actual front door, wearing one of his polo shirts and sweatpants. But the entryway and his whole apartment looks like it's covered in plastic sheeting. Clearly, they haven't finished the redo of the apartment.

My grandfather has his red toolkit out and he's fiddling with one of the front doors.

"The door hangs down," he says to us by way of greeting, "and so the door doesn't close correctly."

He is super tall, like me, and has white hair with a little bit of blonde still in it, and a fast-sharp smile that I like, where he flashes white teeth and then closes his lips in a kind of satisfied way as if to say *that was a good smile wasn't it*?

He sees Jackie and says "Hi! I'm Hans."

I wonder what name my friend will use. They seem to retreat a bit and find a compromise.

"My name is Charlus, but my friends call me Jackie."

"Hello Jacky," says my grandfather, extending his hand. "Why don't you kids come into the kitchen while I fix the door."

The kitchen! That's fine because now I really do need to eat supper, and the sandwiches are feeling less and less appealing (especially since they're probably hot now and smooshed from jumbling around in the backpack), and I'm thinking I would like some of my grandfather's signature bacon and eggs.

Yes, he's a Jew who eats bacon. Because bacon is delicious, even though it is mosdef not kosher.

I also like the kitchen because it has these amazing paisley upholstered chairs that used to be office chairs so they are on wheels, and you can roll around the entire kitchen and never have to stand up to get a spoon or something and that's really fun.

"*Dieu*," says Jackie. "*Comme elles sont laides ces chaises*!!"

It's true. They are extremely ugly chairs. Grandpa picked out the fabric himself after Grandma threw him out, and he was so proud of this green and orange with a touch of bright pink paisley fabric that he selected without anyone else's input.

He has terrible taste. Along with the chairs, the apartment is full to the gills with chandeliers because one of my grandpa's friends owns a chandelier store and sold them to him at a deep discount.

And the terrible taste is just another reason why I love him.

"Come on—sit down," I tell Jackie, as I pull some threads off the arm of the kitchen chair. I roll them up and stick them in my bag, so

Grandpa won't see that the cloth is pretty crummy, as well as pretty ugly. And we plunk ourselves down and wait for him to stop "fixing" the door.

We look at the TV which has professional wrestling on.

I swivel in my chair, smiling. I am thinking about the bacon and eggs and the fun times I used to have with Grandpa. He is very into professional wrestling and he has taken me a few times. I am thinking about a guy I saw once in a town called Reseda. We sat in a really gross hot old gymnasium and watched a guy wrestle there who reminds me, now that I think of it, of the faun. His name was Carson Alpha. He's what they call a "heel," but he is so angelic looking that you know he isn't really bad … he's just pretending to be bad. My great aunt Betty has seen him fight and she says that he's really a shy boy from Canada and that it's all acting. I love that—that I don't really know who he is, and that all that he is showing us is pretend.

As Jackie removes their Converses and gives them to me to put back in my backpack (because they really don't go with their outfit), I start explaining to them about baby faces, and heels, and about how professional wrestling works, and how it's of course all pretend, but it takes real talent to make it look real, making it actually a quite exquisite art form when it isn't all screwed up by the Weird American Wrestling Associates which is such a creepy right-wing monopoly TV company, Grandpa says.

Jackie looks at me dumbfounded and I can tell from their expression that they don't want to hear about any more weird-ass American pop culture—although this is now, thanks to the internet, quite an international phenomenon, but really could we just have some bacon and eggs?

Grandpa comes back in and starts getting out the frying pan and the eggs, which I believe is a good sign.

He starts asking us about school—parents and grandparents always do that, but when Grandpa does it I don't mind so much because he is just trying to be polite and make conversation and for God's sake what should we talk about—sex and dating?

So, I tell him about *Twelfth Night*, and I tell him about what a mess the house is, and then I lead my way up to asking if we can both stay with him for a while, because to be honest we could use a change of scenery, and could he please show me what he knows about fixing things?

"*Monsieur* Anfang," says Jackie. "We understand that your beautiful apartment is undergoing *quelques réparations....*" (I wish Jackie would stop trying to talk to parents and relatives whom they don't know in this pretentious way, but what do I know?—I'm not European or continental like both of them are—I mean Jackie and my grandpa).

"Well," says my grandpa, "and by the way Jacky, call me Hans." (He's VERY cool about having young people call him by his first name.) "Let's not worry about that just now. Let's have some food, and let's relax, and let's just take our time with all this."

"It will be so great, Grandpa!" I say. "Like when Mom and Dad were separated and I came and lived with you for a while, remember?"

He doesn't answer, but on the other hand I smell the eggs cooking and they're great, and I'm hoping there's cheese in them because I like cheese, and then I notice something.

"Where's the bacon, Grandpa?" I say

"I don't have any," he says. "I'm trying to cut back. Salt, fat, cholesterol."

"But you're really skinny!" I say, and he is—he's really thin.

The phone rings—he has this funny old-fashioned black dial phone like in *Superman* or, once again, like *Perry Mason*.

"You kids relax and eat," he says. "I'll take this in the bedroom."

......

"You don't have to," I say but he's gone, and he's left the eggs in the pan still cooking, so I roll over in my chair, turn off the heat, and split the eggs evenly on the two plates.

"À boire," says Jackie.

I roll our plates over to the kitchen table, roll back to the fridge, and take out cans of Sprite.

And there's the bacon tucked away in its usual spot.

"That's funny," I say.

"What is?" says Jackie.

"Nothing," I say. Because maybe he doesn't want to use up all the bacon from the Bacon Club, which I did last year with my friend Belinda before she moved to the Bay Area, and Grandma got so mad at Grandpa for not reminding me not to eat the Bacon Club bacon, although man was it tasty. And I wonder if that is part of the reason she made Grandpa move out: people are passionate about the Bacon Club.

We eat our eggs and watch the wrestling show, but through the yelling and selling I can hear Grandpa trying to speak quietly (but he's always a bit loud). "Yes, they're—Really? Do you mean it, because if you don't. I don't know … And will it be soon? Because it's hard and I can't I can't really, and I actually feel—."

"Let's look at the bedrooms," I say because I don't want to listen to him arguing or having some kind of very intensive personal convo with a perhaps new girlfriend. "Let's figure out which one of us is going to sleep where."

We walk past the plastic sheeting into the first bedroom. It's a sea of beige and chandeliers, except for a huge painting that depicts my grandfather's life in miniature stages like a giant comic book all on one big canvas.

In the first little picture, there is my grandfather in Frankfurt as a tiny child, being picked up by the woman with the plumber's toolkit.

And in the next little square he's out in San Diego as a kid in the 4-H Club growing big stalks of corn. And then he's doing various things like marrying my grandmother. And there is even a square that shows my grandmother lying next to a burning motorcycle looking NOTHING like what she actually looks like, gazing adoringly—or as adoringly as a tiny comic book figure in a very brightly colored painting by an admittedly quite nice Jewish lady who wears wild hats and has a gallery in Oakland (I met her once) *can* gaze—at my grandfather while he holds her hand or what I think is her hand, because in this rendering it looks more like a lobster claw, only very small. Then there's a picture of my father getting his law degree and there are other boxes where my six various uncles are doing genius things with their equally genius-y children: fixing noses in an operating room as a child watches raptly; flipping potato pancakes for the Yankees in a huge kitchen as a child watches raptly; demonstrating martial art moves to a class wearing a gold medal as a child raptly punches another child opponent; sitting at computers with numbers on them as three children play raptly with an abacus; and playing a clarinet and the harp at the same time in a theater, as two children sit in the audience clutching a toy piano and a tiny violin. Raptly.

At the bottom of the huge canvas, there's a box with wrestlers wrestling, and there's also a picture of me as a child playing with my parents in an itsy-bitsy sandbox.

"Was the artist high when he made this?" asks Jackie.

"She," I say.

Jackie smiles and ducks their head slightly. Of course, it's strange how sexism really infiltrates us. We still tend to think anyone important is a man.

There is a slight coughing behind us. We turn around and Grandpa is standing in the doorway. It's one of those wide Westwood doorways with double doors, which explains why we see the other people standing next to him.

Next to him are two people wearing blue and white polo shirts with the Star of David on them.

CHAPTER 11

Wait—it gets worse.

Behind *them* Jackie's parents are standing, and next to THEM is an elderly woman who must be Jackie's grandmother.

"Sarassine," my grandpa says, but he's immediately interrupted by Jackie's mother who starts yelling things like:

"Why didn't you phone, Charlus? Where have you been? What is that crazy outfit you have on and where are your shoes?" while the father, who is wearing a fancy black suit with a purple tie, just stands quietly next to her shaking his head.

"*Opa*," I say, because that's German and I'm trying to get him to focus his attention.

But he ignores me. Looking at me and ignoring me—that's possible isn't it? Yes it is because he's doing it—

"Sweetie," he says, looking somewhere between my forehead and hairline, "these nice young people are here to bring you to your Jewish Wild Child Wilderness Camp in time for Shabbat."

"Hello young Jew," says the one person in a blue polo shirt. "I'm Noah and this is Tamar, and we're going to escort you to the Simi Valley version of the Holy Land in other words Haaretz, where you can get in touch with your identity, all while learning how to chant from the Siddur, sing the Israeli national anthem acapella, and learn some junior life saving."

This is such a weird speech that Jackie's parents stop talking and the father says, "*Quoi?*" which means "what," and that's kind of not a bad reaction if you think about it.

"Grandpa," I say to him, grabbing his arm. "Did you already know these people were coming, and is this why you hid the bacon?"

He closes his eyes for a moment.

The Camp counselor girl—Tamar, I guess—takes my other arm. The Noah man gets between me and Grandpa and he takes my arm and holds it.

I try to get away from them, but they hold me tightly and tell me not to struggle.

This is beginning to remind me of the time the private investigators grabbed my friend Brianna when her and me and Jackie went to the movies at Century City.

"Grandpa, what is this?" I say.

Grandpa opens his eyes and looks at me—finally. His eyes are pale green, and the blonde strands of his mostly white hair make me think that these features may be why they—the Nazis—didn't give him such a rough time when he was at preschool in Frankfurt after Hitler took over.

"Your grandmother called," he says, "and she says — she knows—."

I get it now. Grandma called him when we went missing. And then she called again, promising him something or probably threatening something or both so he would help her out.

My cell phone rings. Noah and Tamar let go of my arms, so I can get my cell phone out of my backpack which is right where I put it on the kitchen table so I can't leave the bag somewhere or have the phone fall out of my pocket or something.

It's my dad, at last.

"Dad!" I say. "Please come get me at Grandpa's! I'm—"

My dad sounds tired but he's a lawyer so he's a good interrupter.

"Sarassine," he says. "You're going to have to move out of the house, because the pipes that run under the house are rotten and the floor needs to be taken up and the water will remain turned off until it's all fixed."

"I know that, Dad," I say. "I called Mr. Pasternak! And the situation is completely under control," (it isn't, and I know he really doesn't like Mr. Pasternak, but it's impressive that I took that initiative, and I'm betting that my Dad hasn't gotten home yet, so he doesn't even know what things look like), "but Grandma came over and she got" (I search for a Dr. Gregorian term) "HOSTILE and so that's why me and Jack—I mean Charlus are at Grandpa's—we—"

"Just listen," he says. "I'm in the middle of an important de-brief I mean conference, and I can't talk for long."

"Please come to the condo," I say. I look at these increasingly grim looking parents, grandparents and the two J Crew-threw-up-in-here college students wearing those terrible polo shirts and truly ugly cargo shorts. I can hear the crowd booing the wrestlers in the background.

"I can't," he says. "And neither can your mother. We're—dealing with something."

And I think to myself *yeah, they're like getting a divorce right now, or doing something like that, just like Grandma and Grandpa.... Why can't anyone in this family stay together, and if they can't, why did they get married in the first place, for Pete's sake?*

I'm about to just ask him "Are you getting a divorce?" But he interrupts that almost question AGAIN and says the following:

"Because of this house situation, we're sending you to the Wilderness Camp that your grandmother recommended!"

Fuck—he's talked to Grandma. They've ALL talked to Grandma.

"DAD—NO!"

"You'll be safe there you'll do a little learning—you'll eat well, you'll learn junior life saving like I did as a boy."

I feel cold and hot. Jackie is lifting their hands to me, for "what is up?" while their grandmother is whispering to their parents something probably disparaging about American children and how they have absolutely no respect for their elders.

"But what about school, Dad?"

Everyone stops what they are doing at that point, because what teenager ever in the world said, "but what about school?" in an attempt to reason with a parent?

It's a startling situation.

"The advantage of private school is one can make these arrangements."

I remember about my dumb-ass role in *Twelfth Night*, and suddenly I think Sir Toby Belch is the greatest guy ever and Shakespeare is a genius.

"But what about my part in the Shakespeare play!"

There's a shuffle of voices, and then my mom gets on the phone.

"Sarassine," she says. "Don't worry. It will all come out in the wash."

Then she just hangs up.

The Tamar woman puts her hand over my mouth.

"Don't do that," my grandpa says, and he puts his hand on her other hand, which is on my arm, and for a moment, I think he's going to stop them.

"OK, sir" the Noah man says. "But please—it's better for the intervention if you don't uh intervene."

Jackie shouts "You're kidnapping her!"

And the woman says "we don't use those terms here. This is an intervention and we have been trained and certified by...."

They start "ushering" me out the door. In other words dragging.

I. Can't. Believe. It.

Then I say something to Grandpa that I admit is extremely mean and that I am certainly going to regret but at the time I completely mean it.

"COLLABORATOR!" I shout.

Tamar and Noah drag me out the door, and I can see that Jackie's parents are doing something similar all the while apologizing to my grandfather but in a way that makes it sound like they blame him too.

❓ Words with special meanings for Jewish people

A "**collaborator**" is someone who works with the bad guys in power—like the Nazis—or who just goes along with them because it's easier and seems safer. Sometimes, the collaborator can also spy on and rat out anyone who might be resisting. See https://en.wikipedia.org/wiki/Collaborationism See also "Collaborationism", The American Heritage Dictionary of the English Language, Fourth Edition

---

Then they start nattering at Jackie, "You need to get ready for the play," they say, "and your *grand-mère* is here to visit us and not have this kind of distress, and the less that's said about this cross-dressing the better."

"I'm not—" says Jackie.

But that's all I hear because Noah and Tamar have successfully pulled me out the door and into the elevator. We go down, past the lobby floor, into what I guess is the basement, and we go to a big black SUV and then they "escort me" into the back of it, and Tamar gets into the driver's seat, Noah riding shotgun.

We sit silently in the van. Tamar takes us onto the freeway, which is a strange expression when you think about my particular situation. An unmarked bus with blacked out windows drives next to us for a while. If I were feeling better I would wonder who was in there, but I am not so I don't.

Traffic is light. And in Los Angeles terms we get to where we are going pretty fast. That's to say in about an hour.

It's dark, when we pull into someplace.

Then they pull me out of the car.

"Welcome to the Baruch Bardot Torah Study Reclamation Retreat Center for Wayward Youth," Noah says.

I see two giant candles lit for Shabbat.

And there's an enormous Israeli flag flying overhead. In the distance I can still see the lights of cars on the freeway.

And right in front of me is a huge campfire, with a bunch of people sitting around it, singing.

Faces look up, and the crooning stops.

"Here's our new camper!" shouts Noah. "Let's sing out a hearty Baruch Bardot welcome by doing a final round of the Israeli National Anthem before we hit our bunks."

I take a seat next to a bunch of dark figures who I can't see very well, but since they are small and slumped over and manifesting total boredom (unless they are roasting marshmallows [which some of them are doing and I am {as usual} hungry again and wondering how I can get some]), I am guessing that these are other kids, which I guess is some comfort.

As I try to remember how *Hatikvah* goes, I remember something.

Before I was forcibly removed from Grandpa's apartment by insane Israel-loving quasi-kid-kidnapping camp counselors, I DID hear one exchange.

Jackie saying, "Can I at least use the bathroom before I leave."

And my grandpa saying, "OK, but don't flush. The pipes are all stopped up. There's trouble below."

"Psst, is that you Sarassine?" says someone. The figure squats next to me by the fire, as a few people get up to go find their cabins.

"Hi Brianna," I say.

 Would it kill you to learn a little history?

"Hatikvah" is Hebrew for "hope," and it's the Israeli National Anthem, adapted from a poem written a long time ago by a guy in Eastern Europe (Ukraine, I think). The poem talks about the longing in the hearts of all Jewish people for the land of Israel, and the hope of moving back there. I don't really understand this, because I live in a place with palm trees and a desert already, but some people—especially our grandparents and people their age (but sometimes younger people too)—are really passionate about it, unless they feel the opposite, which some friends of my parents do. It's actually a pretty song. See https://en.wikipedia.org/wiki/Hatikvah

---

CHAPTER 12

I don't know about you, but I have always found it strange that a group of people who were herded into shacks in the middle of nowhere, forced to do awful labor outside and then were murdered, and thrown into a ditch (at least at the beginning), have such a love for being out in the country and doing camping. Even if actual camping can be admittedly the OPPOSITE of the concentration camp—like it is in the movie *Defiance*, where a Jewish group lives in a forest in Poland for like five years and builds a synagogue and teaches university courses and does dentistry and gives concerts and all the other stuff that they say they did there—fine, but WHY REPEAT THE EXPERIENCE?

After three weeks at Baruch Bardot, I can say pretty much with confidence that we seem to be recreating the *Defiance* movie in SoCal, which is funny if you think about it for two reasons: 1) because we're here as a punishment because WE were the defiant ones (just saying); AND 2) because probably some of our parents were involved with the production of the film (Hollywood).

We're living in cabins and we're learning how to build fires (and then sit around them and sing songs [and roast marshmallows when available]), and how to recognize which berries are poisonous (most of them are, and anyway this is SoCal and there's not really any vegetation to speak of), and how to do a racing dive into a pool and how to save someone's life if they're drowning. We also run a lot.

And … the food is frankly a disappointment. Vegan. Don't get me started.

On the positive side, we're such an odd assortment of kids that making friends feels pretty easy. And I knew Brianna already and she introduced me to everyone else.

Have you noticed how if you can just meet that first person you are like good to go with everyone else somehow?

And I start to fall in love a little bit. Maybe.

With a girl called Hannah White (it used to be Weiss, but her family changed it when they escaped Austria, because they feared the anti-Semitism in the US [I know, I know]), who knows how everything works in this place, and who has already shown me where the books and game shelf are in the main lodge so we can keep ourselves sort of entertained, which is sort of our responsibility because:

1. There's no internet, and they've taken our phones.

2. No one really does any Jewish learning here. The Hebrew teacher got fired right before we came, and the rabbi never shows up, so we have free time when we aren't running, swimming and doing camp craft. Noah keeps reminding us that we all have to be very fit because we will probably have to join the IDF when we make Aliyah, which of course we will want to do, and let's all light candles and sit around the campfire and sing Hatikvah one more time.

Since we don't have much supervision after hours (because the counselors spend their evenings around a campfire smoking weed), we play Star Wars Monopoly, and we look on the shelves in the lodge for whatever books we can stand. I find a huge book which has all the plays of Shakespeare. I take the whole thing back to my bunk and I'm reading it before taps, which is—of course—another round of *Hatikvah*.

Another odd thing is that everyone at camp except for Hannah and Brianna thinks I'm gender-queer and trying to transition to being a boy.

How did this happen? In the melee at Grandpa's the convo got

Oy gevalt, you don't know the IDF?

Just kidding. I didn't know what it was either until someone explained it to me. The IDF stands for the Israel Defense Force which is the Army, Navy, and Air Force all rolled into one thing, and I think everyone has to serve in the IDF if they're under a certain age. I remember riding on the metro once with Jackie and hearing a woman explain to a man who was clearly kind of trying to ask her out that she'd been in the Israeli Army. "I bet you know how to shoot a gun," he said kind of flirting. She nodded. "And fly plane," she added. He looked stunned at this, and I really wanted to hear the rest of that convo, but we had to get off and go to Universal Studios. See https://en.wikipedia.org/wiki/Israel_Defense_Forces

confused and Tamar and Noah got the stories switched between me and Jackie. This is wrong, of course, but the good thing is that instead of being mean, all the counselors are being very UNDERSTANDING and open and kind to me because as long as you're pro-Israel, pretty much anything else goes here in terms of gender orientation and identification as they call it. So, everyone is asking me all the time what my pronouns are and since Sarassine is so hard a name to remember, I have everyone calling me Sam.

And by the way, it's "he, him and his."

I feel sort of uncomfortable about this story because at least some of it is a lie (I don't [think I] want to change my assigned sex), and because I think I may be doing something called "passing," which I admit kind of bothers me.

OTOH, this acting like a boy is pretty cool. I like wearing an undershirt and t-shirt and trunks for swimming, and I like feeling boy-spacious, boy-powerful, when I walk around the camp with Hannah. It's great NOT to feel like that mute masturbating girl in *The Shape of Water* or, worse, that girl who's so flipping passive and scared all the time in *Pan's Labyrinth*. When I see Brianna and her boyfriend Justin, he kind of salutes and says, "hi bro," and that feels great.

......

75

So I feel my swagger when I walk around camp with Hannah over to the cafeteria and to the art studio and to the main assembly hall.

We're not seeing Brianna that much because she's hanging out with Justin and HIS friends. So, it's mostly me and Hannah with my secret, and she has already said she thinks *she's* bisexual anyway, so I can swagger and act like a boy all I want 'til I figure it out.

Yeah, I take to it.

And I like pretending to be a boy with her. Or maybe the word is "presenting."

"Where ARE we anyway?" I ask Hannah one afternoon. We are both sitting in my top bunk and our legs are dangling off the side, and bumping into each other sometimes, which makes us laugh and then one of us runs our leg up and down the other person's until it gets too shivery. Then we laugh and try something else.

"Who cares?" says Hannah. "We don't have homework, and the household chores aren't too bad, I guess."

I blink at the household chores comment, because all we do here is make our beds, and then take turns emptying the trash and sweeping.

"I need to know," I say, "because I'm really thinking I should run away for real, because I don't have a house to go back to and I don't want to deal with my grandmother, and I have no idea WHERE my parents are."

(I haven't heard a word from either of them)

Hannah nods.

"We're in Bel Air," she says. "Well, technically, we're in Simi Valley, which is just thirty miles away, as the crow flies."

Esther, who is one of the disabled campers, and who is here because she just stopped going to school and rolled her wheelchair over to Roxbury Park where she spent her afternoons reading Nietzsche, says, "It's really not bad here."

......

"I know it's not *so* bad," I say. "But still, don't you want the freedom that the freeway promises?"

"Who told you that?" Hannah says. She has stopped swinging her legs and is now tickling the back of my knee periodically.

"No one," I say. "I just mean that we like live in this famous place, Southern California, where everybody wants to come for the freedom, and so why shouldn't we have that or at least a part of it?"

"Well, we *are* right near that fancy hotel," says Esther. "We could sneak into the spa over there, maybe."

"I'm sick of spas," says Paige, whose mother owns two spas in Westwood.

That's when Rusty, the one boy (cis-gendered, that is) in our bunk pipes up.

"I have a question—is Baruch Bardot founded by the same people who founded Diamond Bar?"

Hannah looks at him across the room. He is attempting to sweep the floor and not doing a great job of it.

"Well, because they both have 'Bar' in their names."

"No, dummy," Hannah says, "'Bar' means 'son of' in Hebrew. What kind of bar mitzvah did you have that you don't know that?"

"I was bar mitzvahed at the Postmodern Ethical Culture Jewish Institute of Atwater Village," Rusty says with what I think my mom would call *gravitas*, which is Latin for seriousness and fanciness. Then he gets back to work.

"Wait," I say, looking out the window, stopping the leg game which has been a mutual thigh-tickling competition, for a moment. "Isn't Simi Valley still part of LA?"

"Practically," Hannah says. "You haven't really gone anywhere. You've just changed neighborhoods."

"Diamond Son..." Rusty intones over and over again, as his broom

......

tries and fails to catch the dust kitties that skitter across the floor.

I laugh, and then Hannah takes my hand and then I just lean over and kiss her right there on the bunk in front of Rusty and Esther and Paige.

"Argh!" everyone yells. "Get a room!"

Now that I've had my first kiss, here's more info about Hannah.

She's thin and fast and energetic and intense. We're the same height, which is cool. She plays clarinet and practices every day. She can play Brahms and fancy shit like that. She has enormous self-discipline, and she can canoe and hike and row and swim for hours.

"Endurance," she says. "Life is about endurance." I guess she feels strongly about this because her father died of cancer recently.

"Teach me," I say to Hannah.

So we start training in the pool when there's a free swim. She starts showing me what she learned in Junior Life Saving from camp last year. It's hard for me to learn, of course, but she's amazingly patient; she shows me over and over what to do. She takes my arms and lets me feel the gestures. It helps.

I start swimming laps. A lot of laps.

She's not only faster but much stronger. I give out much earlier.

But as the days go by I get better at swimming. In arts and crafts we do the usual really old-fashioned stuff: we make lanyards out of that plasticky ribbon stuff, we make mosaic plates that I imagine were once ash trays. It takes me a long time to understand the instructions on how to make these things, but no one minds. In the evenings, I start rereading *Twelfth Night* and our bunk takes turns with the book, reading out the parts. We just go around in a circle, except for the quick dialogue bits, and then two people hold the book and read with maybe a third person looking over that person's shoulders. Viola is still my favorite and I would like to play her for real someday. She swims and lives while all the others drown. And she pretends. To be a boy. And she wins out and gets the other woman in the play to fall in love with her AND she gets the husband-duke at the end. Not that a husband-duke is the be all end all, but I mean she's happy. I mean she's not alone.

I think about Jackie pretty often and wonder what they are up to. I think about how messed up our parts were in *Twelfth Night* and how Jackie really should have gotten the starring role of Viola and I should have gotten the part of her somewhat clueless twin brother Sebastian. Thinking about the play and about my wonderful best friend helps me feel better, and I need to resort to what Dr. Gregorian calls "wholistic methods" because my meds have run out, and the counselors won't renew scrips without special arrangements with parents, so I'm feeling a bit fractured and a bit anxious. And a bit something else.

Like I said, it's almost fine.

Today Hannah shows me how to pull a drowning person who's fighting you out of the water.

"They're desperate," she says. "And desperate people have no morality. They'll do anything to stay alive, including KILL YOU."

"They're bad, you mean."

"No," she says, "but they're so afraid of dying, that they climb on top of you and choke you even though that will kill you both, and even though you are trying your best to help them."

"I don't understand," I say.

So she gets in the deep end of the sectioned off part of the pool and starts thrashing. I swim out to her, but before I can grab her body, she puts her two hands around my throat and pulls me down.

For a moment I think she's really going to drown me. I push her, but she's stronger, and I feel myself blacking out.

"See?" says Hannah as she pulls both of us to the air. We're gasping, and I can barely tread water.

"Fuck," I say. "What do I do with someone like that?"

"Get away first, save yourself first. Then you got to get mean and fight them into position to be saved."

"And if I can't?" I say.

"Then you leave them and try to go find help. Don't forget that lesson."

When someone holds you under water, you learn how fast you can drown.

"I suffered with those I saw suffer," says Viola in *Twelfth Night* about the shipwreck that brought her to the strange island where Duke Orsino lives.

Did she try to save anyone as she swam to shore? I wonder. *Shouldn't you at least try?*

At night I'm so tired from the running and the swimming and the camp craft where we whittle for Israel and we make lanyards for Israel, and the endless Hatikvahing, that I fall asleep as the stars come out.

It's all pretty good—aka almost fine—until the power outage, which happens after the earthquake, which is coming up in this story pretty soon.

But before that the showers start acting up.

And before that the toilets stop working.

And before that, Hannah leaves.

One afternoon, I come back from swimming laps, and she's gone.

"Her mom says they have to deal together with mourning Hannah's dad, and so they're going on a vision-quest type trip," Rusty explains. Sweep sweep.

I run out just in time to see the car pull out. Hannah's profile turned ecstatically towards her mother.

"Are you sad, Sam?" Esther asks.

"Yes," I say.

And by the way, where the hell are my parents?

That night I'm getting ready for bed, Rusty announces "the toilets won't flush again."

"What do you mean 'again'?" I say.

Esther says, "let's go talk to the CIT in Cabin #2. He—Zack—says he has a message for you."

"Let's go!" says Paige. She's bored.

"OK," I say, "Let's go talk to Zack. But first I have to pee."

"Yay" says Rusty. "This means we can pee in the woods like the proverbial bear."

"You mean shit," says Esther, but he's already off and running outside with a roll of toilet paper.

So, we go out after him into the brush—this is California, folx, and so there's no woods or anything—with flashlights, and toilet paper, and I pee behind a bush, and then Paige pees, because why not? And Rusty pees, because it's easy for him and then we go to cabin #2 for our appointment with Zack. Esther doesn't pee, because it's a bit more complicated outside, and she says she doesn't need to.

While we're peeing, Esther fills me in on Zack, who is on the spectrum, and is here at the camp for troubled kids because he apparently refused to study or do any of the math problems at Forked Roads Progressive School, and so he's here being intractable, and at the same time—supposedly—teaching us Camp Craft. Mostly he sits in his cabin and plays *Dungeons and Dragons* with his younger brother, who is not on the spectrum, but just wanted to get out of town.

"No, you CANNOT be the Dungeon Master this time," Zack is saying to another boy who—I guess—is the brother. "I have the entire story figured out in my head and—good," he says seeing us. "We need more players."

"But I WANT to practice being Dungeon Master," says the other boy. "And I too have an entire story-line in my head and, I'm sick of being a half-elven bard."

"Then you need a new flipping character, dude," says Paige. "And Zack, give Oscar a chance to be Dungeon Master. Or are you embarrassed to admit in public that your own character is a tiny cleric girl gnome, who is secretly in love with a dragonborn?"

Zack blushes. He likes Paige. Obviously. It looks like it's mutual.

"So it's *you*," he says to me. He ignores Rusty, who kind of gallops over to him and keeps on shifting from foot to foot hoping for some attention.

Zack's brother Oscar sits quietly, organizing some sheets of paper. Rusty gives up and plunks down next to him, and starts asking about how *Dungeons and Dragons* works exactly and is it anything like the Settlers of Catan which he has played with his older cousins.

"Greetings Zack," I say.

Zack pushes his glasses up his nose, reaches under his bed, pulls out a deck of tarot cards and starts laying down on the bed next to Oscar. "Are you perchance the releaser of the pipes?" he says to me. "The unstopper of sewers. The susser outer of sanitation?"

"Is this like the old *Matrix* movie?" Rusty says. He jumps up, grabs their broom and starts sweeping.

I just look at Zack. It's just too weird. PS—this kind of IS like the *Matrix*.

Zack continues flipping over cards and looking at them.

"So are you going to pull the cookies from the oven and tell me I'm not the one or what?" I say.

"That reminds me," he says. He leaves the card and leans over the other side of his bunk. "Here," he says, hefting something. It's a bit hard to see in the not such great light of the cabin. "My therapist, who comes in from LA, and who knows your therapist—a Dr. Gre-

......

82

gorian—gave me this to give to a camper whose last name was AN-FANG. That's you, right?"

I nod. Put my hand out.

It's a shopping bag with something that doesn't really fit inside. Like an umbrella or something in it. I can tell from the feel.

"And there's a message too," Zack says. "Look inside."

I take the bag and feel around the long pole-y thing for an envelope that says FOR S. ANFANG on it.

I open it.

Fancy heavy stationery. I have to squint a bit, but I can read it OK:

James Gregorian MD, Ph.D. Diplomate,
888999 Westwood Blvd
Los Angeles CA 90887

Dear patient/Sarassine-

I understand you've run into some trouble with the law, which in Lacanian terms almost always means the father, but in this case seems to mean your candy-chomping, motorcycle riding grandmother and her attending pre-post-Zionist zealots. Your parents are delinquent on their bills but rest assured that I will help you to the degree that I can. I understand you are not getting your meds regularly, as substances are heavily controlled in your environment, which is typical, unfortunately. On the other hand, I've been meaning to take you off your dyspraxia meds on a trial basis, because they tend to impede certain adolescent developments. You may now begin to feel things. This may prove surprising and uncomfortable, but it is necessary for adults—even and especially urban adults living in the early Twenty First Century—to feel and deal with emotions. But perhaps this humble implement will help you bring what must be brought up to the surface.

I look forward to seeing you again, and am until then very truly yours—

James Gregorian, MD, PhD. Diplomate.

Zack starts telling me how uninteresting I am, but he's interrupted in his speech by Tamar, who is in charge of this bunk.

"What are you kids doing here screwing around at this time of night?" she shouts in a hoarse voice, trying to cover up the fact that she hasn't been here because she's been outside with Noah—who she likes, but who doesn't like her because he likes this other girl and so there's all this jockeying for position and they do all that in the counselors' hangout area which is off the cafeteria. So she comes in all dilated eyes, and weird expression, trying to look like she hasn't been getting high which of course she has been. We ALL know what that looks like and she isn't fooling anyone.

"Look counselor," says Paige. "Zack gave Sam this Nordstrom's bag so he can make a WE LOVE Israel collage out of it."

"OK," says Tamar, trying not to cough.

Seriously, it's weird how lax security is in here, once you're IN here.

Tamar walks us back to our cabin and I open the Nordstrom's bag.

Inside is a wrapped package. HAPPY EARLY BIRTHDAY, it reads.

Inside of it is a plunger.

CHAPTER 13

The next morning, I march off to the toilets with the plunger, and since it's so boring at this place, a group follows and watches while I try to make it work. See, everyone here is so privileged that they've never had to fix anything, let alone deal with a toilet. So the plunger is a mystery to everyone—even Tamar and Noah, my original abductors, who you would think would know stuff but don't know anything and who therefore show up to see what the commotion is about.

I get Tamar to google a YouTube video of how to use a plunger on her phone, and she shows it to me. I have to watch it like 5 times, and even then, I'm not sure I get it. But what we do collectively figure out is that you have to create an airtight seal around the hole that everything goes down. I finally do that, and I PLUNGE.

If you've ever plunged a toilet, you know that it makes a weird sound, like a reverse belch. The sound is soft, because you're covering the noise, and the disgusting water comes up around the rubber mouth I guess you'd call it of the plunger, as the toilet groans. But it comes up and you flush. Then you do it again. Sometimes it takes three tries but in my plumbing experience—which is still small at this point—three times, like in a fairy tale, does it for (most) toilets.

I do one, and then the next one, and then the third one and then the fourth and the fifth. There is a muted *Yasher Koach* as well as an "OK, time for breakfast," and we

> **?** **"Yasher Koach" is both Yiddish and Hebrew for**
>
> "Good Job!"

return to our regularly scheduled program of not very much.

There is something about it—this fixing things. It makes me feel good.

So, I start looking around for plumbing problems to fix, and looking for an actual way out of this place.

My next plumbing challenge arrives almost immediately after the toilets. This is when the shower heads in the bathroom stop working, and so I borrow a stool from the kitchen, and ask Paige to spot me (because my balance isn't so great [dyspraxia]), while I look at the holes where the water should come out but is just dribbling. The holes look kind of white and crusted over like zits. "Clogged," Paige says, who isn't quite as much of a spa girl poser as I thought she was. We go get Rusty to help us. R. is really OCD, because in addition to sweeping all the time, he keeps on picking up cigarette butts and smoking them, which is terrible for you as well as disgusting. OTOH he has very strong hands and is pretty agreeable, so under my supervision (and of course Tamar, who is supervising in her "I'm not from Santa Barbara, I'm from *Montecito*" way) he unscrews one showerhead from the shower pipe. And then we soak it in some warm water.

We put it back on, but nothing happens.

Esther has an idea. "Showers are like sprinklers," she says, after the soaking attempt fails, "and the gardeners know all about those."

So I get permission to skip arts and crafts and go talk to them.

Yes, we're in a desert, but since this is a Jewish camp, of course there's a formal garden off the parking lot complete with lawn, shrubs and roses. Don't ask me.… It's a SoCal thing.

Something else that's interesting: when the gardeners are outside working, there are these kids with them. Not kids who go to our camp. Other kids. Most are tiny. A few are older. Two of them help with the actual gardening—a girl and a boy. They look to be around our age.

In fact, I am seeing a lot of non-camp kids running around the campgrounds. If I had more headspace to think about this, I would, but I have to concentrate on my plumbing DIY apprenticeship and on (maybe) getting the hell out of here.

The gardeners shake their heads at me when I approach them; they don't want to be disturbed. But then I show them the shower-head. Tremendous discussion in a language I don't speak. Then they start talking at me. The girl and the boy ignore us. She clips hedges. He rakes.

I mime water coming out of the shower head.

"No," they say.

One of the cooks comes out. A super-tiny child comes out with her, holding onto her skirt. I show her the showerhead.

"That's easy," she says. "It's calcified. Try soaking in vinegar." So I go with her to the kitchen and get some vinegar and we soak the showerhead in a bunch of warm water in a stew pot.

As I stand at the sink observing the soaking process, I notice more non-camp kids in the camp kitchen. Little ones. Sitting at the kitchen table coloring. They went kind of rigid when I first came in, and one kid leapt out of his chair and scooted under the table. But the cook made a hand signal at them. Now they just keep coloring.

I take the showerhead and head back to the cabins.

Rusty screws the showerhead back on and voila!—The shower works. We do the same with the other ones.

We settle into a routine.

Rusty sweeps with great joy from morning 'til night and Esther learns recipes that feed large groups from the cooks she's made friends with. Paige spends more and more of her time at Zack and Oscar's cabin, playing D&D with them (she explains to me that she is an aggressive, but helpful half-Orc), until very late at night when

Noah or Tamar make her go back to her own bunk to sleep.

The gardeners garden and then go back to the cabins where they apparently live all year. The cooks also seem to live here all year long. I still see the little non-camp kids. But except for that one time in the kitchen, they run when they see me.

But not the older gardening kids. They don't run. They keep weed whacking and lawnmower pushing when I come around. They hoist big garbage cans of branches and leaves and leftover grass from the lawn. They run hoses and then they wind them back up into big green coils. I wave at them sometimes. They seem nice, and they're working a lot, not hanging out like the rest of us are, and I guess I want to say "thanks for taking care of the lawn and the trees and the shrubs and the decorative succulents," but I feel weird saying that to another kid, so the wave stands in for those feelings. The girl smiles and waves back at me. She has very long, beautiful black hair that she tucks behind her ears when she waves. The boy waves sometimes too, more hesitantly.

And I start talking to the rest of the camp about being careful with water, and not using so much toilet paper, and trying to respect the equipment.

I wait.

I'm used to waiting. Jackie and I used to spend a lot of time waiting for things. We'd wait to talk to the school counselor, we'd wait to for our parents to come pick us up. Or we'd wait for frozen yogurt. Or we'd wait for the bus. We'd use the time to talk about our favorite stories.

"My favorite stories are about transformation," Jackie said. "Like that old movie *Legally Blonde*."

"There's no transformation in that," I said. "You just like the outfits!"

"And the dog," they added. "And the boyfriends. They're all cute."

Now that Hannah is gone, there is absolutely no one here who I would call cute.

CHAPTER 14

With Hannah out of the picture, I guess my closest ally is Rusty although to be honest, he's nowhere as interesting as Hannah was.

He keeps on talking about *the Matrix* all the time, and it's annoying.

"What if," he says to me one night, "this isn't the world we think it is?"

"I don't care," I say.

"There's a play I read called *Life is a Dream*, and in it a guy is imprisoned in a dungeon because—"

"I don't care either," says Esther.

"Me three on not caring a rat's ass," says Paige. "It's boring here."

July Fourth comes and goes and so does Bastille Day and Rusty is still wondering about the fabric of reality and Paige and Esther don't care and I keep on nagging everyone to conserve water. And NOT drink from those single-use plastic bottles.

"We live in a desert, you know," I tell Paige and Rusty as we take a rest from our field trip where we've been put in a van and taken up into the hills where there's an olive grove, and we are picking olives JUST LIKE IN ISRAEL.

"I've heard that the Palestinians won't let the Israelis grow their olives in peace," says Paige. "I hear that farming is so hard, because the Arabs are always picking on the settlers."

"It's the opposite, you numbskull," says Zack. He looks around to make sure the counselors aren't listening. "It's the Israelis who bully the Palestinians—it's like the Israelis are the capitalists and the Palestinians are the proletariat."

"The what-i-at?" says Rusty, filling basket after basket with olives.

"No," says Esther, "it's like the Israelis are the Germans, and the Palestinians are the—oh wait, that's not right...."

Oscar interrupts. "None of this matters, because what we are is stuck HERE."

We all look at him. He NEVER talks!

"We need to get out of here," I say.

"But how?" says Esther.

"Easy," says Paige. "I'll drive us."

CHAPTER 15

The question is where, and the destination issue preoccupies us as I use my plunger regularly and urge campers to take shorter showers like the IDF does. I'm making that up, but I'll bet it's true.

We use lights-out time in the bunk to plan the escape.

What about money?" I ask the olive-pickers.

"I have an Amex credit card," says Rusty, "and my parents are exploring the Arctic currently, so they won't check the charges."

"No," Paige says. "We need cash."

"And—" Oscar says, "it would be useful if we had one adult ally." Everyone is silent thinking about that point.

"I don't know about allies," I say. "I thought my grandfather was my ally, and he was just...." I don't use the word "collaborator," but I think it.

But while I'm not saying what I want to say, the others all say:

"Oscar—what are you DOING here?"

"I snuck in," he says.

"How the hell did you do that?" Paige says.

"The magic book," he says.

"Wow," says Rusty. "This really IS like *Harry Potter.*"

"Shit, Oscar—cut it out," Paige says. "And how old are you anyway, Rusty?—fourteen or four?"

Esther pipes up, "Everyone knows there's no such thing as magic, especially in Judaism!"

I say, "Come off it, Oscar—you're small and you came in before we did, and you hid under the bunk, right?"

There is no answer.

We turn on our flashlights and beam them around.

Oscar is gone.

"What a weird kid, even by our messed-up standards," Paige says, and we fall asleep.

I remember something.

Grandma's book.

The next day, I go into my backpack that's under the bed. *Practical Kabbalah for Total Schlubs* is still there in the backpack, and the pack is next to the trunk that got sent to me a few days later filled with gender neutral camp clothes (Grandma's work again, I presume, because they look like hand-me-downs from my dad and uncles).

I haven't thought about the book since I took it. Also—I don't want to read it because reading it makes me think about Grandma and Grandpa, and my parents who have not written or called or visited or anything, and so I'm having what Dr. Gregorian calls abandonment issues, and just thinking about it makes me really mad, to be honest.

I'm so mad I swim more laps than usual, and when I practice lifesaving with Tamar, who's being the fighting drowning person, I kick her in the stomach before dragging her to the edge of the pool.

"Sorry," I say.

"Actually," she says. "That was perfect. That's just the right thing to do."

We lie down on our towels.

"Are you OK?" Tamar asks. "You know—I overheard you guys talking about appearance and reality and what if the world wasn't real."

"It was just an idea," I say to her.

"Yes," she says. "I believed in God once." She sighed and looked at her yellow nail polish. It's pretty, that nail polish.

"And then the God idea—well, it just goes away."

I wouldn't know as I've never had the God-idea. But plenty of people do, and it must feel really good to have it and it must feel really bad when it goes away. I can see that. If I had more time I'd ask her about it, but I don't.

I go over to the lodge and pull out a paper map from the shelves that they've got there for the counselors of yesteryear who used such things to drive around.

A map of Los Angeles County and vicinity.

It's enormous, and we actually have to lay it on the ground outside the cabin to look at it.

"This is ALL LA?" says Rusty.

"Yes," I say, "it also includes Santa Monica, which is technically a separate city, but it's really still part of LA."

"We need space for four people."

"And it needs to be wheel-chair accessible," says Esther.

"What about a loft downtown?" says Paige. She knows downtown well, because that's where her stepdad's law firm is.

We are talking about all this outside when Tamar shows up again.

We quickly roll up the map and start talking about superheroes we think are sexy.

"I know what you guys are up to," says Tamar.

"I told you," I say. "We aren't up to anything!"

"The fact is," she says, "we counselors hate it here too. I'm just doing this because I lost my work-study at UCLA, and things aren't going so well for my parents' business, and I—well I thought the work would be easy."

She looks at me.

"But what happened with you, Sam—" she sighed, "I felt like what we did was like a covert CIA thing. I felt kind of like a terrorist."

"I think you mean Homeland Security," says Zack, who happens to walk by.

Tamar looks around at us.

"But I'm really responsible for all of you!" Tamar says.

"Actually you're not," says Oscar, who has once again appeared out of nowhere in a way that I'm beginning to find creepy. "But you DO have authority to order and execute emergency evacuation procedures for children, should the necessity arise—it says so in the counselor bylaws."

"I can't believe you actually looked that up," I say.

Oscar shrugs. "I've memorized the entire manual—I did it before we even got here."

"Why ARE we all here, anyway?" Paige says to Tamar.

"You are here because you are in trouble at school behaviorally or academically or both and/or your parents don't know what to do with you and/or they are going through something intense like a life-threatening illness or a divorce proceeding, and so the camp was modeled on one of those wilderness adventure places where they take you forcibly if you are a drug addict or involved in anti-social and or self-destructive behavior."

I nod. I've heard of those places. Jackie knew a girl who got woken up in the middle of the night and abducted to someplace like Colorado.

"But this place is considerably less hard-core," I say.

"Well, duh," says Rusty. "We're Jewish."

We all look at him. That has got to be the smartest thing he has said yet.

"It's true," says Tamar. "Jewish parents don't roll like that. So we abduct you, yeah, but then when you're here you just get a lot of exercise and learn to swim, and do Israeli kinds of things, in case you decide to make *Aliyah*."

📖 Nu, how about some more Hebrew?

"Aliyah" means "ascent" in Hebrew. So, "making Aliyah" means "going up" to Israel (why it's "up" Idk), if you're a Jew, because if you're Jewish you're not going someplace new, you're actually returning to your homeland, which is why all Jews have something called the "right of return." See https://en.wikipedia.org/wiki/Aliyah

---

"I'm NEVER making *Aliyah*," Zack says. "Israel is a dangerous and boring capitalist state that has betrayed the socialist promise of the kibbutz system."

"What happened to the actual learning part of this place?" I say. "Why aren't we studying Torah?"

📖 Nu, a little more Hebrew

"Kibbutz" means "gathering" in Hebrew and it was this cool way of living in a group where people farmed and lived and raised children together and it sounds' like an actual, really amazing summer camp, only it was people who really lived like this all together all year long in Israel starting I think in the early 20th Century but maybe it started earlier. I guess you'd call these collectives, and so they were kind of socialist-y, or what I guess socialism is supposed to be. I think, though, people aren't doing this so much anymore, and the kibbutzim (that's the plural) are more like company campuses, and they manufacture technology and other stuff. See https://en.wikipedia.org/wiki/Kibbutz.

"Our teacher quit, right before you guys showed up," says Tamar. "So, we use the Simi Valley junior cantor and the junior rabbi from Simi Valley synagogue to come do the religious services part. But they are on summer hiatus."

"So maybe, that's why the director didn't hurry to find a replacement for the

Hebrew teacher," says Esther.

"We had a Hebrew teacher?" I say.

"I remember her!" says Rusty. "From last summer!"

Oscar says, "After all, the Torah is not so simple a text. So maybe you don't want kids who are a problem thinking too much about what good and evil are and whether or not God exists and why there is so much injustice in the world and what does the sacrifice of Isaac mean from a kid's point of view."

"So—maybe the Torah/Hebrew teacher made the kids think too much," Esther says.

"And then there's the Holocaust," I say. "How can a God-idea ever fit in with that?"

The guy that Tamar likes comes along, raises his eyebrows at her, and she walks off for another campfire pot-smoking meeting.

"How many years have you been coming here, Rusty?" I ask.

"Every year," he says. "As long as I can remember."

"Why?" I say.

He shakes his head. "Maybe I'm not really here, and this is all a dream, like in that play."

We decide that Oscar and Zack can come with us, if we can find a car big enough.

That night when the others go to sleep, I get Grandma's book out.

One of the things my mom taught me is to always look at the table of contents before you start trying to make your way through a big book.

PRACTICAL KABBALAH FOR TOTAL SCHLUBS

I close the book and put it back in my backpack.

CHAPTER 16

That night there's an earthquake.

It's not like the famous Northridge quake our parents talk about, and it's not the big one that everyone predicts is going to happen. It's minor.

But it's enough to wipe out the power temporarily and make what's left of our plumbing completely messed up.

So, we're up and at 'em early after a quick mournful morning rendition of *Hatikvah*. And since the camp is broken, arrangements are made—in a typical lackadaisical fashion—to transport us all up the road to our sister camp in Santa Barbara, which is at least in another county and is cooler supposedly, both temperature-wise and attitude-wise.

We quickly make adjacent plans over cold cereal and milk distributed by the counselors, as Noah talks on the one remaining working cell phone.

Where are the rest of the phones? No idea. No one does.

I pack the backpack I had with me when I was abducted. It still has the Gucci slingbacks in it with the broken heel, as well as Charlus' clothes. I don't want to leave them behind. And the stupid book of Grandma's.

Still not one word from my mother. Or my dad, but somehow that bothers me less. No letter. I mean I've heard from my flipping THERAPIST but not from my mom. I'm mad. These feelings, man. Wow. Is this why Grandma is so pissed off all the time? Damn, if you got all these emotions swirling around all the time AND you're old … well, I kind of get it.

The counselors are packing up the kids and loading them into a bus. I see Brianna get on the bus with Justin. I wave to her, but she doesn't notice me.

My last connection to Sarassine.

Tamar waits with us 'til the end when we're the last group and she's going to drive us. We get Esther and her wheelchair loaded into a van.

Room for eight people.

"What are you going to do with Tamar?" Zack asks me quietly as Tamar loads the wheelchair.

"Why me?" I say to him.

"Because," he says. "You think you know everything, so let's see you deal." He steps forward and tries to stand over me. He's tall and does this looming thing that's really irritating, because I'm just as tall, so I stand up straight and loom back.

But I also realize that we need—if not an ally—then a moment of cooperation from a grownup.

"Listen, Tamar," I say. "Now's your chance to atone for the wrong you did me and my friend at my grandfather's and—I know it's not Yom Kippur yet, but you have this one chance, right now, to make reparations."

My heart starts pounding and I realize suddenly that I'm actually really mad at her for her part in the summer camp intervention thing at Grandpa's condo.

Then I remember a plot point from *Twelfth Night*. Sir Toby and Sir Andrew play a trick on the guy who runs the house. They play a practical joke on him. It's mean, but they get away with it.

Some have greatness thrust upon them. That's the line.

"I don't know," she says.

"It'll be easy," I say. "All you need to do is pass out, and then tell the truth. We tricked you and took the van."

"How can I pretend to pass out?"

 The most intense spiritual day on the Jewish calendar (it happens in the fall, sept or oct)

"Yom Kippur" is the day of atonement—or as my mom explained to HER (now dead) mom, "it's kind of Lent and Easter rolled into one day minus Jesus" (this is what she said, literally). So you fast—no eating or drinking from sundown the night before 'til sundown the day of YK—and think about all the crap things you've done during the past year and if you've done something wrong to someone you are actually supposed to ask them for forgiveness, and you try to forgive the people who've wronged you although if they haven't apologized you kind of don't have to forgive them. Anyhow, you spend the day in synagogue praying and feeling hungry and thirsty and you do activities and conversation, and then some more praying and then you have a fantastic meal of cheese types of food because they are easy to digest. Like bagels and quiches and omelets and stuff like that. https://en.wikipedia.org/wiki/Yom_Kippur.

While I've been talking, Zack has been fiddling with his toiletry case.

Zack hands her a cup.

"It's Motrin pm, four doses," he says smoothly. "It's fine. Our mother's a pharmacist," he says. "You'll be fine, unless you have taken cold medicine or have been drinking."

Zack looks at me and winks. So, I guess *we're* allies now, even though we find each other a pain in the ass. And I wonder how he managed to keep the Motrin stashed. He's a sneaky one.

"Our mom does this all the time," says Oscar. "She says she doesn't know what hit her and she doesn't know what happened to the car or the kids or the money or the whatever." He produces—out of thin air—a can of Diet Coke.

"And remember," Paige says, "You're just a volunteer! You can't get sued! It was an emergency! It's in the bylaws, right Oscar?"

Oscar nods emphatically.

Paige gets in the driver seat. She sits on a cushion and props herself up.

"Where are we going, exactly?" she says.

I show her the map. "We're going to go to Santa Monica," I tell her. "We'll live on the beach with the other homeless people."

"I'd rather go to Portland," says Zack. "It's cooler."

"It doesn't matter," says Rusty. "We'll have each other. Like in *Peter Pan*. The lost boys, although we're more the lost girls and boys and nonbinaries."

"Wait," Oscar says. "There's a problem!" We all glare at him.

"—what about our parents?"

Shit—we forgot about that.

"Yeah," I say. "We're going to need to fake our own deaths."

"WHAT?" shouts everyone except Paige who is sitting in the car grimacing.

"You guys," she says. "I need silence so I can concentrate. This car is BIG. Backing up is going to be hard. So please shut the fuck up."

Tamar opens her mouth to say something, and suddenly I remember what Grandma said to me and Jackie. It was like German only not quite, which means it was Yiddish.

? The least you need to know!

to get people who hok you a chinik to shut up is to pronounce the following words while waving your left hand:

zey shtil!"

"Hang on, I have to look something up!" I open up the book and search for SILENCING.

I point at Tamar and say those words to her. Tamar opens her mouth, and then points at her throat. The spell worked: she can't talk.

Next, she holds out a printout with camper names on them. She has crossed off most of the names as the other kids have gotten loaded into the bus and cars. But our names are still there.

Then I remember:

Fun with the alphabet....

Everyone else gets into the van but me and Zack. Tamar looks at us, nods, and tosses back the Motrins with the help of the Diet Coke.

Zack takes the printout while I flip through Grandma's book,

```
The hue of the writing provides the crucial
clue. The color of the print (blue or black
ink) works with the Lord of the Universe (the
paper or screen). Without these two forces
working together you would never comprehend
the creation story, nor would you be able to
understand what that narrative means for you
personally.
```

```
For an extended discussion see our companion
text ZOHAR FOR TOTAL SCHLUBS.
```

```
    Short cut: Say
```

Farshvind

```
    and wave your right
    hand
```

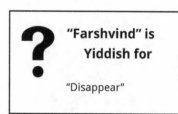

"Farshvind" is Yiddish for

"Disappear"

I speak and wave and our names start to fade from the printout that Tamar is holding. The lines shrink the space and the font squiggles and wiggles to match so everything looks like there's nothing missing.

Rusty yells from the back seat "Is it working? Like Harry Potter?"

"The office," Zack says to me. "The computer."

I walk into the office.

"**Farshvind**" I say to the keyboard on the desktop computer.

The alphabet and all the numbers disappear. Qwerty isn't qwerty anymore; it's just smooth blank keys that look like dark chocolate squares. The exclamation mark and asterisk linger for a second. Then, they too fade away.

I open the drawers in the desk. I grab an envelope with cash in it marked PETTY CASH. I walk back out. I look up. I remember something my grandpa said about when the Nazis came, and I pull the mezuzah off the doorpost. I put it in my backpack.

I run back to the van.

"Does this mean they won't notice we're gone?" I say to Zack.

"IDK, you're the fucking magician," he says. "Get in the car."

Paige shouts. "SHUT UP, please."

We are silent, because after all she IS the driver.

Paige starts the car. We pull out of the driveway sloooowly, as Tamar lies back on the one remaining lawn chair and puts the printout over her face.

CHAPTER 17

We drive.

The problem is though that Paige can only drive very slowly, so we have to avoid the freeway because we look too suspicious, and besides Paige hasn't learned how to merge—why would she?—she's fourteen and learned how to drive in Goshen, Indiana when she went to visit a schoolfriend's aunt, and her cousin's bff took them driving at night for fun, and they smoked cigarettes.

I think she kissed the bff, but she's not talking, and I don't want to ask her.

We drive so very slowly. For I'm not sure how long.

Then, we run out of gas.

"Oh," says Paige. "I forgot to check the gas part. I'm used to driving electric."

Rich kids.

I have regained access to my travelers checks, and we have the cash from the office drawer. But we don't know where a gas station is.

Paige has managed to pull over onto what I guess you call the armpit of the road, and together we manage to push the van into a driveway that says:

B'nai Ahava Retirement Home.

A hand-made sign below it reads: **FM Certified.**

"Oh God," I say, "Not more old Jewish people. They're the reason I'm here in the first place."

We walk up to the kiosk, but there's no one there.

There's a yellow post-it that says "check in here" on a sheet that has boxes for you to put your name, your business, your license plate number and the time you arrived.

"Hey," says Rusty. "Can we just say we're like a family? How about the Finkelsteins?"

"How about the Cohens?" Oscar says. "Generic."

We fill in the name THE COHENS, but use the real license plate, so no one calls the cops on the "suspicious" vehicle.

It's late morning, but the place is really quiet.

The old people must be having like water aerobics or physical therapy or something.

We get Esther out of the car, and we proceed quietly out of the parking lot, and look at the signs for nurse's station, intensive care unit, and recreation center.

"Look," says Esther, "there's a garage over there. They'll have gas there maybe or can tell us where to get some."

"Wait," says Rusty. "How do we explain ourselves as Cohens to the REAL Cohens?"

"Stick to the truth as much as possible," Esther says.

"No," I say. "If you're going to lie and you're a kid you have to go big."

"OK, genius," says Zack. "Let's hear the lie."

What would Sir Toby say?

"I have it!" I say. "We got evacuated from our family compound up the road, and we're on our way to Santa Monica, to get to our aunt and uncle who are in the Industry and who live on the beach."

"Ooh, can they be related to someone cool?" Paige asks.

"No," I say. "They're set designers and cinematographers and lighting people—behind the scenes. Don't get into visibly famous people. That feels like too much of a stretch, and it's easy to check."

"So, we're three boys, two girls and one—what?" says Zack.

"One undecided," I say. Because I still have my Sam clothes on, and I have to remind myself that none of them know that I'm really just Sarassine. And all I've got with me are Jackie's "Charlus" clothes. And at this point I'm not sure I know who I am exactly either.

"Can we all be part of the Cohen family?" Rusty keeps asking.

It's stupid because we don't look alike, but it matters so much to him. And thus the lie gets a bit bigger. More spacious.

"Sure," I say. "Some of us are adopted, and some of us are from the first, second and third marriages. That would explain why we're almost all around the same age."

"Or both!" says Rusty.

"Exactly," I say. "This is Southern California, and anything is possible here with families."

"So that means you keep your real last name, you just add Cohen on to it. Let's sound off," I say. "Be bold."

"Just a minute," says Paige. "I am not comfortable with just adding "Cohen" as my last name."

"Why not?" we all shout together.

"Because I'm not Ashkenazi, my real last name is Shirazi, and my Persian ancestors went through a lot of crap with the Shah to come here."

Nu, what's with these fakakta categories?

Ok, so it turns out that the word "**Ashkenazi**" refers to Jews who come from countries in Eastern Europe—like Germany, Poland, and Russia. Jews from Spain are called "Sephardim" and Jews from the Middle East sometimes identify as "Mizrahi," though Jews have emigrated all over the place and these labels don't always fit the way you might think. See: https://en.wikipedia.org/wiki/Ashkenazi_Jews and https://en.wikipedia.org/wiki/Sephardi_Jews

"What about Cohn-Bendit, the famous French leftist?" offers Zack. "He's Sephardic."

(How does he know this stuff?)

"No, he's not," says Paige. "He's German, but all right—Bandandaz-Cohen, it is."

"Which means...?" I say.

"'Bandandaz' is Persian for 'Plucker of Hairs.'"

We look at her.

"You know—like waxing and threading."

"That's a cool word!" says Rusty, and we're back in business. We all start thinking about what to do with the Cohen name to make it fun and interesting.

"Sound off, please," I shout, now that we've spent fifteen minutes on the last name question.

"Paige Bandandaz-Cohen—first marriage. My mom is a hair stylist."

"Rusty Espinoza-Cohen—second marriage. My mom works for *Cirque du Soleil.*"

"Espinoza?" Esther says. "That's my Spanish teacher's name."

"I don't like to make a big deal about it," Rusty says. "BUT, I'm Latino technically. Why do you think I know all about *La vida es sueño?*"

"What?"

"It means 'life is a dream.'"

So, Paige is Persian, and Rusty is Latino? I squint. I never thought about how the other kids here may not all be exactly white. I mean they're Jewish, so I kind of assumed....

"Spoken like a White person," Jackie would say if they were here.

Esther interrupts my super-uncomfortable line of thinking.

"Esther Kleinberg-Cohen—third marriage. Wow that's a jewy name—my mom is a rabbi."

"Oscar Rothchild-Cohen—fourth marriage. I'm adopted."

"Zack Rothchild-Cohen—fourth marriage. I'm adopted too. We're actual brothers."

"Nice touch," I say. "And you do look alike. Sam Frankfurt-Cohen—recently adopted. My birth mom is a painter. She gave me up because I interfered with her art."

"I like Sam Frankfurt-Cohen," says Rusty. "It sounds like a hot dog maker's name."

I shake my head. Rusty.

"OK—just act mature," says Zack.

"Just speak in a lower voice," Oscar says to me. "That'll make the non-binary thing seem more believable."

Oscar seems to sense my act is bullshit, but I can't fix that now.

So it's time, after all, for the Sir Toby voice.

We walk in the garage, and what do you think we see?

An old lady tied up, hanging upside down from the ceiling.

"Oy," she says, shouts really, in a kind of hard-of-hearing way. "Sid, don't start yet."

And to us, she says, "Hi kids—don't worry—this isn't as bad as it looks."

An old guy man dressed in black pants comes out from behind a very shiny Rolls Royce. He's not wearing a shirt, and it's interesting to see someone that old with big tattoos of snakes and trees and crocodiles running up and down his saggy belly and chest. Also a lot of scarring. Maybe from a war?

"Goddamn it Sylvia—oh," he says as he sees us.

We all stand there, looking at each other. Esther is still sitting, but for the first time since I've known her she's at a loss for words.

Zack squints at them for a moment. Then puts his index finger in the air.

"I saw about this on YouTube."

"What is it?" Paige says.

"I'll tell you later."

I'm trying to figure out what "this" is, when Rusty comes to the point.

"Hi there! We're the Bandandaz, Espinoza, Frankfurt and Rothchild-Cohens!" he shouts. "Do you guys happen to have gas for our car?"

I hold my breath. That's some name we've come up with.

"No, sonny, I don't unfortunately," says Sid as he pulls some ropes and pulleys which makes Sylvia come down from the ceiling and he grabs a hold of her and undoes the straps. I notice that she is wearing a black leather bikini. Or maybe pleather.

Sid wraps her up in a quite nice black bath sheet.

"What's happened to you, *bubbelah*?" she says to me.

Sylvia is a mass of wrinkles and sag. But she has bright blue eyes that twinkle.

It's funny how you think old people are all one way, but in fact they're very different.

I explain that we've run out of gas trying to get to Santa Monica.

"We'll call a council meeting and see what is to be done about you and your van."

"We don't really have time for that—" I explain.

"Sure you do," says Sid. "And anyway it's way past time to eat lunch. What are you going to do, starve?"

It's like 11:45 a.m., but I guess these old people like to eat early.

So we go with them to the cafeteria. All the lights are on, because they have super fantastic backup generators powering everything.

"Now," says Sylvia. "I just want to say one thing before we go in. It's important in life not to get judgmental. Keep an open mind, you

112

young people."

We open the doors and see that the place is hopping with old people. But these are not the old people that you see at a bat mitzvah or a funeral or in a grocery store with a walker or anyplace I've ever been. There are old people wearing leather bikinis like Sylvia, and very tight black pants and no shirt like Sid. And others are wearing bathing suits. At first it's shocking, and then you just get used to it. I've never seen so many old people with so little on before, and it's funny because they are all kind of saggy, which is somewhat gross but it makes you feel better about your own body when you realize that bodies are kind of weird-looking and they just get weirder looking as you get older.

"This is a clothing-optional place," explains Sid. "But we generally put clothes on for social gatherings, and every once in a while, the kids—that is to say, our kids—come visit, and we don't want them to be shocked and we don't particularly want to announce what we're up to to the management company that runs this place."

We grab trays and select our food. There's a lot of it, and it's all fabulous. There's a bagel station and an entree station and a salad bar. We line up behind two ladies wearing black miniskirts with stockings rolled up over their blueish knees and we pile our plates high with brisket and bagels, and we see a dessert table in the distance but we have to go back for that.

We go sit down next to a woman in a brilliant orange wig sitting in a wheelchair with an old man kneeling in front of her on a leash. She feeds him jello with a spoon.

"Hi there!" she says. "I'm Helen and this is Spike."

Spike barks several times and pants a welcome.

Zack sits at the table with an egg salad sandwich and some peas.

"Is that all you got?" I say, between bites of an everything bagel topped with truly spectacular lox and cream cheese (with capers).

"I'm too excited to eat," he says and then turning to Helen, asks, "So, is this an S and M retirement community?"

Sid comes up with Sylvia and joins us.

"Please—Zack is it?" he says. "The term is BDSM and we are open to all the categories that Fet Monde International admits, and we are also gender queer and trans friendly."

He beams at me.

"Sid is trans!" says the woman with the brilliant orange wig, "and so am I!" I look at her. She looks very real-womanish to me. I do look down at her bikini bottoms, though, and I see a big bulge there.

She sees me looking.

"I decided against bottom surgery," she says. "The technology wasn't there to do it, and these days, I'm good with what I've got."

"Me too," says Sid.

"And you're all Jewish?" Esther says, her mouth full of blintzes.

"Mostly. But we accept you if you were married to a Jew, or affiliate in some ways with Jewishness—which includes being a leftist."

Zack has finished his peas and is remaining on point. "What's your position on Israel?" he says.

"We are all pro-Palestinian and pro the peace process!" says Sylvia.

Sid clears his throat. "Well to be specific, some of us think that, but others of us—me included—feel that Zionism did not have to be historically necessary."

"Yeah," says Helen. "In fact—to tell you the truth—there's a group here that—"

"But wherever we are," interrupts Sylvia. "We want to celebrate and affirm the BDSM lifestyle as a completely kosher choice."

"Especially if it involves a good spanking, eh Sylvia," chortles Helen as she readjusts her wig.

"Please," says Sid. "Let's keep it clean for the young people." He points at Oscar. "They're really too young to—."

"Have some more to eat, Cohens!" says Sylvia.

We finish our lunches and help ourselves to the dessert bar, which includes ten different kinds of babka and various ice creams. And then get seconds.

Rusty feeds Spike an ice cream cone.

Esther rolls her chair over to us with two men who she's been talking to, both of them are in wheelchairs, and one has a leather mask on, with zipper opened up so his oxygen intake tube can fit into his mouth. She introduces them both as "Jake."

"Now this is what I call summer camp!" she says.

They are nodding vigorously.

That's when I notice these people in scrubs moving among the diners.

"Med techs," Sid explains. "They're making the rounds to make sure everyone has their meds or isn't about to croak, excuse me, die, and if they are about to, they move them out into the intensive care wing."

"Don't they like rat you out?" I say to Sid.

"Of course not!" he says. "Why would they?"

"Maybe we should spend the summer HERE," says Zack.

I lose my train of thought, because I notice this young guy—a kid really—going in and out of the kitchen—he's stacking dirty dishes and collecting silverware.

He looks up from a tub of dishes and smiles.

It's in this place surrounded by the very old that I see a beautiful boy who looks like the faun from *Pan's Labyrinth*.

CHAPTER 18

"Time for an emergency council meeting," says Sid. He stands up, waves at one of the people in scrubs, and they go get him one of those portable mics.

"I'm calling an emergency meeting to discuss what to do about our visitors."

It's kind of funny how a lot of people just keep right on talking over what Sid says—just like during my bat mitzvah where I basically did my entire Torah reading over the discussions about the traffic on Wilshire being disrupted by the metro construction as well as whether the mayor of Beverly Hills was in cahoots with the hotel developers on Doheny. We're a loud and chatty people.

"What visitors?" says someone else. There is some loud whispering and pointing.

"I call the question," says someone.

"Not yet, Suzanne," says someone else. "We don't even know what issues we're discussing yet."

"I don't care!" says Suzanne, "I don't want to miss *Jeopardy!*"

"That's not on for another four hours."

"Yeah, but...." is the rejoinder.

We're invited to present our case. It's a bit strange trying to explain yourself to a bunch of old people in latex, but we do our best.

I stand up, but before I can say anything, Rusty just starts in.

"Beloved old people, in the spirit of complete forthrightness—we are refugees from the Baruch Bardot Torah Camp for Wayward

Youth up the road from here. The sewage system broke down, and Sam here tried to fix it. They're—I mean he—is a plumber—but he couldn't handle the damage wrought by the earthquake and so the camp got moved to Santa Barbara."

"So why are you here? Were they going to make you walk there without food and water?" asks an elderly man in a black jacket over a hospital gown.

"No ..." says Esther, trying to intervene, and shaking her head at Rusty in as meaningful way as she can.

"Well thank *HaShem* for something," was the reply.

 Nu, how about some more Hebrew?

"HaShem" is Hebrew for "the name." For many Jews, God is too holy to even call "God," so instead people say "The Name" meaning of course the big guy/gal/entity/force. I actually like this idea because it gets us out of the "Mister God" problem and makes God more well, mysterious.

"Listen," I say. "We aren't wayward, exactly. We are just the kids that our parents didn't know what to do with."

"Well," says Zack. "I am SOMEWHAT wayward."

But no one is listening to us anymore. The whole thing has broken down into small group discussions about our camp, which people keep referring to as a "*Lager.*" I know that means camp in German, because my grandpa taught me that.

This is going sideways fast.

"No, everyone, wait," I say LOUDLY so everyone can hear. "The Torah camp isn't like a concentration camp. It's a weird sort of holiday camp for troubled youth, sort of like—"

I try to remember the name of that place back east that my grandpa went to as a kid....

"It's kind of like the—Catskills," finishes Oscar.

"Ohohohoh!" is the response.

"Only—it's like juvenile hall," finishes Rusty.

"What do you mean? Like REFORM SCHOOL?" asks Sylvia.

Paige looks at me, and shakes her head, and widens her eyes. She nods in the direction of the exit.

That's when Esther speaks up.

"I actually think that many of you would understand how we feel," she says. She rolls over to Sid and takes his arm. "Are you here because you want to be here, or because your kids said you couldn't live in your own house anymore and you had to go some sort of home?"

There's a pause.

Esther pushes on. "I'm taking it your silence means a yes, and that's a shameful feeling isn't it? Someone telling you what to do when you're an adult and have been managing your own life and your own business, and your own sexuality." Wow, I'm impressed that she can use that word so simply, like a complete grown up.

She takes a breath and goes on.

"It's a terrible feeling to be told what you HAVE to do, when you want to figure it out for yourself, and you're absolutely capable of figuring it out, if someone would only give you the space to do it. Well—we are all in that situation too. We haven't committed any crimes or misdemeanors."

"Well," Zack says. "Full disclosure. I stole five hundred dollars from my parents to buy a turntable at BEST BUY, because vinyl is really a superior sound."

"What?" shout the two Jakes, "YOU PAID RETAIL FOR electronics!!??"

I put my arm around Esther's shoulder. I'm sort of a guy, after all. I got to protect the girls.

"I think the point is … that we're like you only the mirror image. At the beginning of our adult lives, while you guys are—."

"Near the end," says Sid. "We know."

I bow to him.

"Right—and we have gotten into trouble with our parents—YOUR children—because we are different, or we have problems, or we just happen to be in the way while they try to figure out their own lives."

Zack is nodding at me. I look around the room, and I see old heads nodding too. They get it. Being old sucks as much as—if not more than—being young.

"So we are asking for sanctuary, I guess," I say.

"Until we figure out what to do," says Esther. "We could use your input actually."

That does it. Seventy-five pairs of eyes light up. It's been so long since anybody asked their opinion about anything.

I know how it feels to have your insights devalued. Or worse. Ignored.

"Now can I call the question?!" says Suzanne.

Sid nods and says, "All in favor of harboring these fugitives for a couple of weeks say AYE!"

There's something cool about all those voices—those cracking high pitched, rasping voices giving the acclamation.

Despite my dyspraxia, which I have not been taking meds for, for more than a month at this point, I think I'll always remember that sound.

CHAPTER 19

After the meeting, Sid and Sylvia and Helen (and Spike) and the two Jakes give us a tour of the B'nai Ahava complex. There's an intensive care hospital-ly type place but it's up the road, and everyone here lives more or less on their own with the help of the med techs and other helpers, who pick them up if they fall down, administer their meds, and more or less stand by should they need something.

We walk by the outdoor pool and the main jacuzzi. There are two women in the jacuzzi kissing, and there's another lady lying on a lawn chair with one of those black bikinis and very long high-heeled boots. An elderly man is assisted by one of those orderlies into a kneeling position (he gets two cushions placed under his knees) so he can lick the spike heel of the boot.

"I know what that is!" observes Zack. "It's a foot fetish!"

"Zack," I say. "Stop with the commentating."

These people seem as happy if not happier than my grandpa, and A LOT happier than my grandma. I wonder how they would do in a place like this.

"So Sam," says Sid, "I hope you won't be offended but I'm noticing that you're very effeminate although you're wearing boys' clothes. I gather you're trans or intersex? We're all very open about this here. Is this part of why your parents sent you away? Gender essentialism and transphobia are quite rampant with middle class Jews who are otherwise very enlightened, or think they are."

I don't understand entirely what Sid is saying, but I'm starting to feel a bit weird again about passing as something I'm not. But....I feel like I can't back out now.

"I'm not sure," I say to Sid, as we meander the paths between these bungalow-type little houses. "I guess I'm what you call 'gender-queer curious.'" I remember Jackie saying they weren't that, so I figure that's as good a term as any to use. Because I am curious. And I'm also not sure.

We pass a group of elders sitting in a circle on the grass, passing around a cigarette.

"You've got pot here!" says Zack.

"Oh yeah," says Sid. "We got it all."

Near the circle, there's three guys wearing horse bridles sitting at a picnic table. One of them is organizing white lines of something that looks like chalk dust.

"Hey," says Oscar. "Is that—*cocaine*!?"

"Shh," say the two Jakes. "Not so loud."

"At our age," says Helen. "For some of us, what does it matter?"

"Dude," I say to Sid (yeah, I'm mosdef getting back into boy-char-acter). "What about the cops? What about like—management?"

Sid jerks his head and we walk to the side, where we can admire some very nice rosebushes.

"The truth is," Sid says. "Like a lot of these senior places, manage-ment isn't exactly what you'd call hands on...." He looks around. "I mean the staff come and take care of us, and the urgent care place is run very well—but the actual managers don't come by more than once a month. So—we make independent arrangements with other vendors. We pay them—shall we say— off the books."

"What about visitors?" I say.

Sid looks away from me and grimaces up at the sun. Sylvia puts her hand on Sid's arm.

"Maybe you won't do this, Sam," she says, "but most kids when they grow up, they lose interest in their parents."

I nod. I lost interest in my parents a long time ago, it feels like.

"Are you saying that no one comes to visit you?" Rusty asks.

"Pretty much," replies one of the two Jakes.

I take a deep breath in. I don't know what to say to that.

The look on Sid's face passes and he pats Sylvia's hand and smiles at all of us.

"Being forgotten has its advantages," he says. "We have taken charge of our reality and made it into kind of a Shangri-La."

"Shangri-what?"

He laughs. "Shangri-La is a place where no one ages, where people live forever." He waves his hand around the place. "We're getting as close to that as we can, under the current circumstances."

"And having a good a time getting there!" Sylvia adds.

"Look," say the two Jakes. "There's Victor!"

It's The Faun Boy.

Sid introduces us. "Sam here says he's bi-curious!"

I blush. "That's not quite what I said," I say.

"Not to worry about coming out—bro," says Victor. "This is a place where you can be yourself and not worry about upsetting the relatives." He shakes Sid's hand. "And I really appreciate the job and the money, Mr. Sid," he finishes.

"None of that Mr. bullshit, Victor," says Sid. "It's just plain old Sid." He looks roguishly at Sylvia. "Or Master." Sylvia giggles.

We walk through the rose garden, and past the very impressive health club.

"So—how did you get THIS job?" I say to Victor by way of conversation. My mom says it's always good to start a conversation with a stranger with a "And what do YOU do?" or equivalent.

"Fet Monde does online hiring," he says. "There's quite a senior community there, and they indicated they were looking for help."

"How old are you?" I ask.

"Sixteen," is the answer.

I'm thinking that if he's a kid, how in the world is he allowed to work here, but he sees what I'm thinking.

"I'm a volunteer officially—you know, helping the old folks."

I raise my eyebrows. Wow.

I follow Victor the faun through the maze of gardens and facilities. I try to find something to say, but it's hard, so we end up talking about money. He's saving up for college he says, since funding is so hard to get here in California.

"Do you like Shakespeare?" I say.

He shrugs. "Not so much. I'm not much of a reader. I'm more of a video game person, like I really like single shooter games."

How can he like those? I think.

"OK—" he says. "I got to go back to the kitchen." Then he holds out his hand. I take it. We are exactly the same height.

"Good to meet you," he says.

I put my hand in his to shake it, but he holds onto it, stroking it.

"Such long slim fingers," he says.

I feel a sort of shudder. It's like fear with want with something else that's new to me. Feelings. New Feelings.

"Come on," says Sid. "Let's get you settled in."

CHAPTER 20

Housing Complex Building *Partsuvim* has great glass elevators so you can see the roses when you go up, and if you're on the ground floor, there are private patios for each suite.

It's remarkably beautiful. Vaulted wooden ceilings of a rich brown.

"This is nothing like Hogwarts," murmurs Rusty. "This is BETTER!"

I walk slowly behind the group, still feeling the hum of Victor inside me. Talk about trouble below....

On my left I can hear voices reading out loud in Hebrew, and I can hear clatter.

So they ARE learning Hebrew here after all, I think, and I stop.

There's a half-open door. I stop and look in.

Four people are sitting at tables surrounded by enormous piles of books and scrolls. They are working in pairs and calling out words to the rest. Another three people, more limber than the others, are actually on their hands and knees on the floor, drawing something.

I take a step in.

It's a huge diamond shape, outlined in what looks like chalk. Along its sides and inside the shape are circles—each one is being filled in with a different color. The top (or bottom) of the diamond is a white circle with Hebrew words already written in black inside of it. A man sits back on his heels with a black stylus. He nods at the writing.

One woman with bright blue hair looks up from the floor and

waves a matching bright blue piece of chalk at me.

"Perfect!" she cries. "We've been waiting for you."

I pause. I'm glad I'm not in trouble, but this arts and crafts thing they're doing feels a little weird.

"Come on, come on," says a man sitting at the table. "Are you number eight, or aren't you?"

"I don't know," I say. "Is number eight good?"

"Eight is the number of completion," says the woman with the blue chalk. "Eight are the days for the consecration of the *Mishkan*, our first tabernacle, eight for the celebration of Chanukah, our first great revolt. And eight is also *Hod*, the double emanation which means both splendor and humility."

"That means, we only need two more," says another woman, tiny and frail, bur dressed entirely in very bright red. "We were seven, the number for luck, for *Gad*, creation and blessing, but we need to get to ten to effect the opening."

I'm about to walk in, when Sid grabs me.

"Come on," he says. "Stay with the group."

"Come back!" someone cries and it's such a sad plaintive sound that it kind of scares me almost.

"What are they doing, those people?" I say.

"It's some social club," says Sid. "We got all kinds of them here."

He pulls me down the hall as we follow the rest of the group.

"So how'd you hit it off with Victor?" he nudges me with his elbow and winks.

I look at him.

"OK, Sam, I dig it. You're a cool cat who likes to keep it private, right?" he says. "Once a boy, always a boy—right? We like to PURSUE." He pauses. "Unless we don't. Unless we like to be objectified—which is also fine."

He speaks to me softly. "I envy you, you know—being a young person on the brink of all this discovery."

I'm embarrassed as hell by this, but also, I kind of like how Sid just says whatever it is. He doesn't hold back. He treats me like an adult.

"Yeah," I say.

We all pile into the elevator and go up a couple of levels.

Sid produces hotel room cards for us, and we all get rooms.

Rusty and I share a room with twin beds, and a view of the pool.

The room is gorgeous.

And the bathroom....

There's a toilet and a bidet and a handheld shower.

I go into it and use the products already there.

I haven't been this clean in weeks.

"Yay television," says Rusty, surfing the channels.

I don't have any clean clothes, so I put on Jackie's "Charlus" cargo shorts and shirt. I miss my friend so much! And how I wish they were here, because they would be so happy. This would be their perfect place.

I come out into the bedroom. The TV is on and is showing bunches of kids sitting squashed together behind chain link fences. They all look a bit like Rusty. Rusty is staring at the screen.

There's a tap on the door. I answer.

It's Sylvia.

"It's time for our dinner-dance!" she says.

Didn't we just eat lunch?

Everyone comes back downstairs so we can all troop back to the cafeteria.

I walk slowly behind everyone again. Will Victor be there? If Victor likes boys, then is he going to like me? Who the hell am I now, anyway?

I stop in the hall thinking about my broken sling-back high heels and kind of wishing I could wear them to this thing. That makes me remember the red and white dress I wore at my bat mitzvah. I looked pretty, I have to admit. I don't feel or want to feel "pretty" often, but I did then.

I walk to catch up with the group.

I pass by that same door with the mysterious social club.

I can hear the old people are still chanting in Hebrew and talking in English.

I look through the half-open door again.

The group is still hard at work, but I can see that the design is just about finished. I count. There are ten circles in all: eight running along the outside of the diamond shape, and two inside. One of the two is in the middle. That circle is a bright yellow. It's very beautiful. I want to look at that circle more closely.

I walk in.

"Hey, it's time for dinner, you guys!" I say.

"*Warte*, we're almost done!" says a man at one of the tables.

I help a lady with bright green glasses to her feet. Then I just look. It's really an amazing design. Every circle on the sides of the diamond has been colored in with a different color: besides the yellow and the blue I already mentioned I'm seeing white, grey, black, green, purple, orange, and red. And on top of that is a Hebrew word. The man with the stylus is just writing the last word in the last circle at the other end of the diamond. This circle is different; it's divided into four colors, like a pie. White, red, green, and black. It's hard to read the word because of the partly black background, but it looks like it starts with a *mem*, which is the "m" sound.

Then the tiny woman I saw earlier dressed entirely in red comes over, grabs my hand, and says "Are you in? or not? Make up your mind, for God's sake."

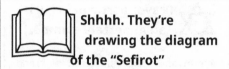
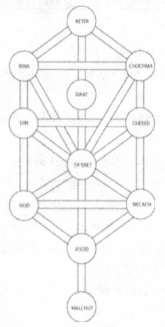
I keep looking at the yellow circle. The color pulses with light and possibility.

"Don't get distracted by *Tiferet*," the woman in red says. "Come in or go out."

"I'm in," I say and go over to sit at one of the tables.

"No—don't sit!" says the man with the stylus.

Another man dressed all in black walks over to the door and slams it shut. Then he walks over to a table, grabs a yarmulke from a basket of them and sticks it on my head.

"Kippahs on, everyone." Everyone puts on a yarmulke, including the women, which is pretty cool (I thought about wearing a yarmulke at my bat mitzvah, but didn't quite dare to).

"We still need two more people," says a third man in a shimmering white t-shirt. "For the temporal opening minyan, which Moses Ben Jacob Cordovero refers to, albeit obliquely."

"Correct: We need ten people for the opening to happen," says the tiny woman in red. "But we can get started with the preliminaries. What is needed now is to prepare the space for the working of marvels, of which correcting past mistakes is number one on the list of things we need to get done."

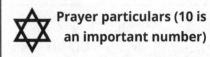

Prayer particulars (10 is an important number)

A **"minyan"** means "number" (I think) and it's the minimum of adults you need to say certain prayers. It used to be 10 men, but now it's 10 adults of any gender unless you're Orthodox, and then it has to be 10 men, which I think is stupid, but I'm not in charge.

https://en.wikipedia.org/wiki/Minyan

"OK, let me check to see what's next," says the woman with bright green glasses. She looks through one of the scrolls piled on her table.

"You're working magic, aren't you?" I say.

"Yeah, of course," says a woman in purple.

"It's time to fill in the *sefirot*," says the woman with the green glasses, looking up from her reading.

"What do we put in the circles?" says the man in black. "Objects or letters?"

"Let's try both," says the lady in purple. More scrolls get pushed around and now little hands made of paper get dumped in all the triangles on the floor.

Now everyone stands up and begins to chant. I don't know the words but I stand by and hum along. We do that a lot in synagogue. You fake it 'til you get to a prayer or a song you know.

"Now—who's going to say the secret prayer of prayers?" asks green glasses.

"The eldest?" says the man in white.

"Or the youngest!" says the woman in red.

The air starts to shimmer.

It gets very hot.

"You!" they all shout at me. Green glasses presses an index card into my hand.

I look at it.

"Are you kidding?" I say. "That's not a prayer!"

"Just read it and stop with the criticizing," says tiny red woman.

I shake my head and haltingly read what's on the card:

"ABRACADABRA!"

A flame shoots out of one of the circles on the floor. More flames shoot up.

Columns of smoke spew out of each fire. They form a huge box of smoke, a house of smoke.

 Who knew it was Jewish? (maybe [or maybe not])

Ok—this is wild, but some people seem to think that "Abracadabra" comes from Hebrew and Aramaic words that mean something like "I will create" or "I do create with the word." See https://en.wikipedia.org/wiki/Abracadabra

"Now bring the megaphones!" shouts the woman in red.

From a corner of the room, two people in black lug over a huge pile of megaphones and puts them in front of the fire.

They are a beautiful color red.

"What's this for?" I say

"To help Bar Kokhba and Rabbi Akiva," Sid says suddenly over my shoulder.

How did he get in here?

"We've got nine!" shouts the woman in purple.

"Another son!" pipes up Rusty behind my other shoulder.

When did HE come in here? The room gets dark. Except of course for the fire.

"Bar Kokhba means 'Son of the star,'" says the tiny old lady in red. "And now we're at ten!"

"The opening minyan will commence!"

"At last," Rusty says. "Real magic!"

The fire burns brighter, and the circles themselves begin to glow like multicolored stars around the fire at their cores.

"Who are Bar Kokhba and Akiva?" I ask Sid.

"Bar Kokhba was, or rather is a partisan," says Sid, putting his hands on my shoulders and gazing raptly into the fire of the *sefirot*. "He and Rabbi Akiva are fighting to win Jerusalem back from the Romans. And they almost do it. We're sending the megaphones back through

---

📖 Badass Jews from the ancient history

Everybody seems to think that when the Romans took over the Middle East that was kind of it in ancient times. They just ruled over whoever was living in Jerusalem and in the land that becomes Israel and Palestine, and no one tried to get out from under the Empire. But that's not true. There was this guy known as **Bar Kokhba** (which means "son of the star" [I think]) and he led a huge revolt against the Romans and held Jerusalem for something like three years, which is amazing If you think about it. Some people thought he was the messiah (yes, Jews believe in one; we just don't believe that Jesus was the one), and for a while they really thought they were going to beat the Romans, because they actually minted coins that have a menorah on them or something else Jewish, I don't remember. Of course, he didn't win, and I think after he was defeated and killed, that's when a lot of the remaining Jews were forced to leave the area. See https://en.wikipedia.org/wiki/Simon_bar_Kokhba

Rabbi Akiva was a famous rabbi who was a supporter of Bar Kokhba's and who I think may have also thought that Bar Kokhba was the messiah, but I'm not sure. He wrote a lot of books, and I remember hearing a story that he danced at his martyrdom, because he was so happy to give his life to Ha-Shem, which is an intense and sad and brave thing to do. He was killed in like an amphitheater by the Romans after the Bar Kokhba revolt failed. See https://en.wikipedia.org/wiki/Rabbi_Akiva

time. So more people can hear them. So they can win over those people who aren't sure, and they can even win over the Romans."

"Wait—" I say. "What do you mean win over?"

"Convert them," says the lady in purple. "Don't forget the batteries for the bullhorns!" Someone adds a box of batteries to the pile of megaphones.

"But I thought it was forbidden for Jews to convert people."

"Not yet," says Sid. "That happens later, after Christianity becomes a majority religion."

"Stop talking!" says someone else. "Focus, so we can finish the incantation. It should just take a couple of minutes, and then we can go eat."

"Wait—no—" I say. The fire gets higher and there's a weird whirring sound, like that time my mom broke the bread-machine that my grandmother bought her for Chanukah because she tried to use the knead function without the paddle and the whole thing overheated and caught fire, and we had to call Mr. Pasternak.

So I raise my voice some more. "Sid—you guys—you can't go back through time in Jewish magic, you can only summon the dead!"

No one is listening so I talk louder.

"Or maybe you can talk to demons or angels or maybe just maybe God! But that's it!"

"And you know this how?" says Sid. Now smoke starts filling the room.

"It's all in my grandma's *Practical Kabbalah for Total Schlubs* book!" I answer between coughs.

"It's working!" the women shout.

Now more flames shoot out of the circles on the floor.

"This isn't the right Kabbalah," I say. "You're doing it wrong...."

Sid laughs and claps his hands. "That's the title of Houdini's book.

The Right Way to Do Wrong. But we're not escape artists, we're trying to prevent the diaspora." He turns to the others. "We love these young people—but sometimes they just don't get it."

He turns back to me. "If Bar Kokhba can retain Jerusalem, then the Exile doesn't happen. There's no issue with the right of return. Because we never left."

Now the smoke around us clears, just as new plumes of smoke spew out of each fire at the base of each *sefirot* circle. Each column a different color. The columns become a giant box. And inside that box, a shadow, two shadows materialize—with smoky limbs that— barely distinguishable—seem to sift through the pile of megaphones.

I stand up. I love old people, but they are really messing this up.

"Let me just go get my *Kabbalah for Total Schlubs* book, and I'll show you," I say to them, in a calm, *I know you guys are completely insane, but I'm going to humor you* kind of voice.

"IT'S HAPPENING!" everyone shouts.

But, suddenly, the fire sputters and goes out. The smoke clears instantly. The whirring broken-bread-machine sound stops. Sid and the others put down their scrolls.

As we look at it, the chalk design on the floor dissolves, the colors and words fading, absorbing the paper hands into the concrete floor. All that remains are the megaphones and the batteries.

"Where's the son of the star?' says Rusty quietly.

"We got really close that time," says the lady in the green glasses.

"Yeah," says someone else. "We'll try again."

"Food time," says Sid, and the entire group gets up and walks out the door, like nothing intense and magical just happened.

The pile of megaphones lies in the middle of the room. People who can't avoid them place their walkers on the other side and clamber over them.

I follow them out into the hallway. But first, I stop. The batteries have come out of the box and are rolling around on the floor. I pick one up. Then I walk out, take the elevator back up to my fancy room, put the battery inside my backpack, and put my pack on my shoulders.

I come back down.

The hall is quiet. I want to go back into the kabbalah room, but I can't find the door any more. There are so many rooms, and all the doors look identical.

I open up Grandma's book. When the table of contents fails, my mom told me, go to the appendix of a big book. That's generally where the cool stuff is.

Appendix on Changing the Past (highly forbidden)

Although not Rabbinically Board Certified by the Kislef Society, a minority kabbalistic opinion in Southern California holds that if the Bar Kokhba Rebellion had been successful against the Romans, Jewish history might have changed in radical ways. The Riverside Rebbe further has argued that the Bar Kokhba bonfires ceremony (currently taking place on day Thirty-three of counting the Omer) should be moved to the day of Tish B'av. This holiday—occurring normally in July—commemorates the fall of Temples One and Two. The Inland Empire/Orange County/San Gabriel Valley learning circle argues that if the ceremony is performed on that day, it is thought that all the destructions might be prevented. For further information see "nonapproved rituals for change" in the Zohar for Advanced Total Schlubs (available as an audiobook only).

I'm about to start looking through the book some more, but Rusty comes charging back into the hallway.

"Wasn't that the coolest thing?" he says. And then, "Isn't this place GREAT?"

I say, "Rusty, they're trying to do actual like forbidden magic here … so I'm not sure this is such a great idea to send help to this Bar Kokhba person."

"I disagree!" he says. "The two Jakes were just saying to Sid that if the Romans never defeated Bar Kokhba, then the diaspora never happens, and so no Zionism, because you know—the Jews never leave. Isn't history fascinating?"

"But Rusty," I say. "If that had actually worked then please explain to me HOW WE would have ended up in Simi Valley dealing with, not one but TWO Jewish summer camps?"

He shrugs his shoulders. Then he grins and just hugs me.

"Sam—you worry about these details too much," he says into my ear. "If you change the past, the present sorts itself out."

"But there's no changing the past!"

"Why not?" he says, letting go of me at last. "Sam—we change the past all the time through the way we talk, the way we tell. Like when I tell my grandchildren about how I ended up in a weird summer camp and then I escaped to an even crazier camp for cool old people, I'm going make every part of it beautiful. Every part is going to feel special and exciting, and I may leave out all the times I felt bored and lonely and depressed and like a complete outsider but I didn't know how to articulate any of that, because I'm not deemed smart in a traditional sense, because as a bilingual learner, I am often judged as not all that great at book-learning to use an expression from *Little House On the Prairie* which I watched once and it's actually pretty good."

I just stand in the hallway and look at him.

"Besides," he says. "I saw on the news that there are really bad things happening now."

"Where? In Israel?"

"No," he says. "Here. Our government is putting kids in concentration camps."

"What are you talking about?"

"What we just saw on TV," he says. "I told you, the world is not as it appears."

"What are you talking about and who ARE you?" I say.

"I'm not sure," Rusty says. "Sometimes I'm just an assemblage of thoughts and feelings. A grouping of emotions."

"I think this place is getting to you," I say. "Or else you're completely brilliant, I can't decide."

"It doesn't matter as long as you're my friend," Rusty says. "Come to dinner."

CHAPTER 21

We walk by the pool and the rosebushes, and we almost trip over a young guy with long hair just lying on the ground in front of the entrance.

"Are you OK?" Rusty says.

"*Ani*," says the man. "*Ani....*"

I know what that word means, and I say the only thing I can think to say and that is,

"*Shabbat Shalom.*"

Then I say, "*Ani Samuel,*" and he says:

"*Ani Shimon.*"

Rusty helps the ostensible Israeli get to his feet.

He looks at me.

"*Anni merapez glida.*"

Like I said, my Hebrew is horrible, but I do know a few crucial words to get around town with.

"Did you just ask for ice cream?" I say to him in English.

"*Ken,*" he says. "I mean...." I see him searching for words.... "Yes—is that right?"

"'Yes' is correct," I say. "Are you visiting someone here?"

"Yes...." is the answer. "And I brought another with me."

"Where are they?" Rusty asks.

Shimon points, and I see another guy lying on the ground.

Bound up in chains.

"Oh my God," I say.

"Don't worry," says the man in chains. "This is nothing. I'll be out in a jiffy."

He starts squirming and shimmies, and in about two minutes, he's standing in front of us, the chains in heap on the ground, wearing nothing but very old looking underpants.

"Uh, are you also visiting someone?" I ask.

"Sure," he says. "If that's the way you want to play it."

"I'm Sam," I say to him.

"Delighted to make your acquaintance, there, Sam. How may I be of service in designing an aesthetically pleasing and audience-thrilling escape plan?"

"We're just going to get some dinner," Rusty says, "so come along and we'll get Shimon his ice cream, and whatever else you'd like to eat."

We walk into the cafeteria with the Israeli and the—I don't know what he is.

The guy who had been in chains shows Shimon how a cafeteria works.

"See—you take this tray and then you just take whatever food you want."

"This is amazing!" Shimon says. "So much food."

Sid comes up and says hello to the two newcomers.

"Welcome, and whom are you visiting?"

"We're visiting you!"

Sid thinks. "I do have some issues with memory loss, but I don't think I know either of you."

"No.... we have been summoned to visit YOU," they both point at me.

"That can't be right," I say. "I wasn't doing any summoning."

"Well," says the guy who had the chains on him. "Someone did something because ... *voila!*" He makes a very expansive gesture like they do at the circus.

That's when Rusty says, "Didn't you use that magical spell word?"

"You mean the *Abracadabra*?"

"Don't say it again!" says Sid. "These guys must have materialized when you said their names and then said that magic word that you just said and shouldn't probably repeat anytime soon, please." He looks around. "So that means one of them must really *be* Bar Kokhba. Where is he?"

I point at Shimon, who has left us to go grab a bowl of soft-serve and a stack of Klondike bars. Which he is now devouring.

"Huh, the ice cream enthusiast," says Sid. "Color me somewhat underwhelmed. We were going to help him to fight, not eat."

"And you are ..." Rusty says, turning back to the chains guy. But he is deep in a convo with the lady in the wheelchair and Spike.

"You know," says the still mysterious visitor, "you could really have more chains on you, and it would look more impressive when you got out."

"But he doesn't want to get out," the lady explains.

"Arf," says Spike.

"But that's the whole point of chains!" the mysterious visitor explains. "You want 'em so you can demonstrate your talent for getting out of 'em." He turns back and I notice that he has somehow acquired a pair of black pants and is pulling on a shirt that he has produced out of nowhere.

"I mean it's all about escape, isn't it?"

He looks at me.

"And you aren't really a boy either, are you? That's your gimmick, right?"

"Now, now," says Sid. "Let's not get essentialist about all this."

"Suit yourself," says Bar Kokhba's companion. He puts his hand on someone's shoulder and from behind their back, pulls out a tie, and a belt.

"How did you get started in this particular line of work?" asks Sid, who—clearly—has gone to the same conversation school as my mom.

"My father was a rabbi," says the stranger. "And nothing makes you want to rebel more than having a papa who is a religious leader!"

I give up at that point and check up on Shimon Bar Kokhba who has polished off the soft serve and has gone back to the ice cream bar and returned with another stack of Klondike bars, two Dove bars, and a bowl of coconut sorbet.

He is chatting with the two Jakes in what sounds like completely fluent English; he seems very at ease here, which is interesting.

"How are you doing over here, Shimon?" I ask.

"Fine," he says between slurpy bites of the first Dove bar. "I'm just glad not to be fighting a battle that we must win, but … that I fear we may lose."

I shiver. This is like *Pan's Labyrinth*. Men fighting because they have to. And girls and women dying in the middle of all of it.

"You—you're not a warrior, are you?" he says. "You look more like a scholar."

"I want to be a plumber," I tell him. He looks blank. Of course. He wouldn't know anything about that.

"Don't you make anything?"

"No," I say, "I fix things."

"What if nothing is broken?"

"Are you kidding?" I say. "*Everything* here is broken!'

Shimon nods as he grabs his spoon and plunges it into the sorbet,

"So nothing has changed. Well, I too seek to repair. *HaShem* says we must attempt it."

"Do you talk to God?" I say.

"Of course," Shimon says. He puts down the empty bowl and unwraps a Klondike bar. "Don't you?"

"I don't think people can do that anymore," I say. "Talk to God—*Ha-Shem*, I mean."

Shimon finishes his Klondike and licks his fingers. "Perhaps you haven't listened closely enough. The voice of *Ha-Shem* can be small."

I shift from one foot to the other.

"So—is that how you know about ice cream—*HaShem* told you?"

Shimon laughs, "Rabbi Akiva saw it in a vision!"

A funny story about a very famous rabbi

According to my dad, Rabbi Akiva was supposedly not the smartest or most talented person. Still, he was determined to learn, so he found a way to do it, at first by eavesdropping (literally) on a Torah studies class from a rooftop. He eventually crashed through the roof and ceiling and landed on the floor in the synagogue, at which point I guess the Rabbi in charge felt he needed to take Akiva on as a student. I think he studied for like twenty years before "getting it." Which goes to show that an inspiring teacher and an important scholar isn't necessarily a genius, which is cool and gives me hope.

I'm about to argue that Jews aren't supposed to predict the future when Victor bounds over to us.

"Hey, who's this?" says Victor.

I introduce Shimon and Victor.

And just like that Sid announces that it's time to dance.

We start with folk dances, and—not surprisingly perhaps—Shimon knows all the steps to everything, the *mayim* (water) dance, and the *hora*.

"This is like home!" he shouts. "Come on! I love dancing!"

Me—I'm not crazy for dancing. Dyspraxia makes it hard for me to learn by watching, and I often feel like I'm thinking one thing and my body is doing something else.

So, I hesitate. I look for Shimon's companion, the mysterious visitor, the one who arrived in chains. He is there walking around the cafeteria, checking doors and windows.

He comes up to me.

"This joint is a bit too small-town for me. Reminds me of Appleton Wisconsin where I grew up. I'm more of a big city person, so—since it looks like you don't need me—I'll be getting going in a moment. I'll see you, when I see you, young man or young lady."

"What's your name?"

"My real name is Erik, and you?"

"I—I used to be called Sarassine, but now—"

"A pleasure." He takes my hand and kisses it. Then he bows, "You'll sort it all out, Sarassine. I just know it!"

He straightens up.

And then he's gone. He doesn't disappear exactly. He kind of melts away. Smiling and waving a length of chain that he has produced out of nowhere, as he does.

Some actual current music comes on.

We dance, or at least I try to. I try to feel the moves rather than just watch them, like lifesaving. I do my best, and before I know it, I'm in a circle with Victor and Shimon.

The circle gets smaller.

I may be not quite fourteen with difficulty with coordination and short-term memory and a dysfunctional family, but I still feel things. This level of wanting is an adult thing. It has a purity to it. A completeness, this wanting. I recognize it and I welcome it.

The music swells and the two of them have me pressed between them. Victor is narrow and tall and hard, and Shimon is hard in a big and substantial way that Victor isn't. I'm held between both of them, and our hips are moving and we're—I guess the word is gyrating. I close my eyes and then I open them, and I see Paige standing on the periphery and I know for a fact she wants this too, and in a way she has as big a claim to it as I, maybe more, and so I reach out my hand and pull her in and now we are four, and then we are five, because Paige pulls Zack into this circle that isn't a circle anymore, and now somehow it doesn't feel right to me anymore. Because Paige and Zack know who they are and I don't, because they aren't pretending and I am. Because Paige is the real deal girl and I'm not. I'm a some kind of something pretending to be a boy, when I'm not even exactly a girl, and I can't make anything and I can only fix things for short term not for long term, and what the hell good is that? I slip away under the arms of these boys and this actual girl, and I walk away by myself to sort myself out, because sometimes, I just feel inadequate to the situation.

Sometimes, it all feels wrong. Then it happens. Paige and Zack kiss.

And Victor and Shimon kiss. And for a moment, I feel like I'm falling, and the room spins. I'm in a place that is hot and smoking where I can hear men yelling, and metal clanging, and then I'm back here.

The music is still going, but the two guys have slid away still locked against each other and Paige who wanders off with Zack, arms around each other.

I remember my mother saying, "This party is for grown-ups," when I tried to join a cocktail party they were having, and my mom had forgotten to give me dinner, so I came out of the television room and kept on asking the bartender they'd hired for olives.

I grab my backpack and I walk out of the cafeteria with all its promise and sex and kisses, I walk past the old people, and the dead that I have somehow summoned, and my camp friends, and I just start muttering "fuck."

I wish I had a toilet to unstop. Something, anything, I could fix in this broken world.

I wander around those palm tree lined paths.

I get a little lost. Like in *Pan's Labyrinth*. That damned stupid movie.

And I end up back outside the suite complex. Not too far from the forbidden door, which I can now see is open as I look through the glass of the lobby. The door to the kabbalah room, where Sid and those other old people are trying to make history unhappen, which is crazy, and which didn't work, but I wonder if they will keep trying. Maybe Shimon will help them. Maybe he'll stay for a while before fading back into wherever he faded in from.

Sid is standing in front of the complex. He's everywhere, that old guy, who realized at some point that he was a man, and not a woman, and who had the guts and the desire to manifest who he really is.

But there are two more people standing with him. The outside complex lights are burned out there for some reason. But still I can sort of see. A tall guy and a shorter guy with flashlights.

"You don't want to go in there," Sid says. "That won't solve our problem."

"Well, what will, asshole?" says the shorter guy.

I stop in my tracks. That sounds like a young voice. A very young voice.

"Listen," says Sid.

"No, you listen," says the other guy. Another voice. Also young.

Now we're both listening.

"If you don't pay for this shipment, there will be problems with my supplier," says the shorter guy with his weird raspy teenage voice.

"I can't make the payment this time—because we've had some unforeseen expenses," says Sid. "And some of us have had issues cashing our checks—the kids, you know. They get—."

"Old man, your financial stress with your kids is not our problem," says the taller guy.

"And it's not just this shipment," says the shorter one. "You owe us for two orders, and we have to keep the supply lines open here with management."

And I know from movies and TV that I've walked into a drug deal.

I step behind a big bush and hide. It's a rose bush and that move is just as uncomfortable as it sounds.

I review my situation. I think about that girl in *Pan's Labyrinth*.

One of the things I don't like about that girl is she isn't very active. She's kind of a pussy if you want to put it in a crude way. She doesn't DO enough to fight that horrible guy, who is like a Nazi stepfather or something. I suspect the older masturbating girl in *The Shape of Water* will do something, but I didn't see the whole movie, so I don't know what she was going to do.

I remember something.

I've been bat mitzvahed and that means I'm technically an adult.

I realize something else. I *like* Sid. He and the others have actually been kind to us and to me. They actually did NOT sell us out.

So—I know you're not going to like this part of the story, dear reader, but....

I walk back.

"Hey Uncle Sid!" I cry out to him as I walk over to them. "That party is a total loser and I'm sad!" Which is kind of true.

A flashlight lands on me. Someone grabs me.

"Look what we have here," says this guy. It's the tall one. Even taller than me.

"Sorry, man" I say, in my best Sir Toby voice. "Just trying to find my way back to my grandpa's suite and saying hi to Uncle Sid here."

The smaller guy keeps talking.

"Let's stay focused—Mr. Saperstein, we have a situation here. You have commandeered our services and we've come all the way out here from Hancock Park."

And I think.... *wait.... who are these guys.*

A light comes on from an upstairs suite. The cleaning staff are leaving and are arguing in some language I don't understand—another one—and the shorter guy's face gets lit up.

He's very young looking—he looks as young as me.

Super skinny. Blonde curly hair, blue eyes. Kind of angelic.

"What are you looking at?" he says to me.

I'm thinking he looks kind of familiar. Like someone who went to my school. But graduated. So genius-y, he graduated early. Went someplace very hard to get into.

"Nothing," I say.

"And you, what are you supposed to be?" says the tall guy.

Cooper, I think, *the tall guy's name is Cooper:* he was friends with Jackie's cousin. He's a drug dealer. He didn't go to college, but he's like in art school or something.

It's weird how everything with Jews is like six degrees of separation. It's a cliché but it's true.

"Sam," I say. "Just Sam."

"You're kind of pretty, Sammy," says Cooper.

Cooper is the muscle, I think. So that must mean that the shorter guy is the brains of this operation.

"But I prefer women," says Cooper, "older women actually, with a lot of cash. So being cute won't help you—it'll just piss me off."

"For Christ's sake he's just a stupid kid," says Sid. "Let him go find his grandma or whoever it is he's visiting."

"He?" says Cooper, "He?"

"But it's after visiting hours now, isn't it," says the shorter guy. "So what's SAM doing here still?"

The forbidden door opens onto the hallway.

"Hey—what's in there?" says the shorter guy.

"Nothing of interest," says Sid.

"That makes it sound super interesting Sid," says the big guy, Cooper.

"There's nothing of value in there," says Sid, and I'm thinking that I don't want these guys getting into the crazy kabbalah room and taking whatever that power might be in there and what it might mean. And I'm thinking that I never actually *do* anything, I never take a chance on anything; things just happen to me and I play pretend all the time, so I'd like to finally actually make a choice about something....

Cooper starts to walk into the lobby.

Sid takes his shoulders.

Cooper does not care for this and knocks Sid down which isn't hard because he's like 100 years old.

 Bracha Basics—the "Sh'ma" or "Shema":

This is a super-important prayer, that you are supposed to say a lot, but especially before you die.

It goes like this:

Sh'ma Yisra'eil Adonai Eloheinu Adonai echad.
Hear, Israel, the Lord is our God, the Lord is One.

Then you whisper this next part to yourself, so no one can hear but you:

Barukh sheim k'vod malkhuto l'olam va'ed.
Blessed be the Name of His glorious kingdom for ever and ever.

See https://en.wikipedia.org/wiki/Shema_Yisrael

And Sid starts to say the *Shma*.

As I keep telling you, I don't know a lot of Hebrew, but I DO know that's a prayer you only say in very serious situations—like when you're in shul or when you are about to die. You do it when you're really scared. I saw it once in a Neil Gaiman comic.

"Wait," I say to the big guy—Cooper.

He grunts and drags me back.

He reaches behind him and pulls out a gun.

And I think to myself *well this is a stupid way to die.*

Almost fourteen pretending to be a non-binary wannabe plumber in two different Jewish summer camps getting shot by a drug dealer.

"I'm going to shoot your queer great nephew Sid."

"No!" I say. "He's not my relative—I mean—I'm not—."

I'm stuttering because I don't want that gun to go off.

"Hey, listen—" I say. "I have some cash as well as traveler's checks."

The shorter guy bursts into laughter.

"Cooper—hold up. We got TRAVELER'S CHECKS!"

He leans on the door, pulls out his own gun, laughing so hard he's bent over the door handle.

Some have greatness thrust upon them.

"Listen—" I say. "I'm not visiting anyone here—I snuck here from the camp, the Torah Camp for wayward Jewish youth. I—ran away."

They are both looking at me, trying not to laugh because it is a pretty ridiculous story.

I open up my backpack. "See—here's all my cash and the checks are in there too—and if that's not enough—my grandpa's rich, and he lives in Westwood. He lives in a big condo, and there's cash and jewelry and TVs and stuff there."

"What do I look, like?" says Cooper, "A fucking burglar?"

"No," says the shorter guy. "You look like an unsuccessful and untalented sculptor." He stops for a moment, thinking.

"But if we take the kid with us, these geezers won't call the police or their private security or whatever they got, will you? We'll dump him somewhere in Los Angeles."

He turns to Sid, who is still lying there. "But if you phone in, man, we'll hurt this kid. We will, or I'll find someone who will, because I can do that. I have those sorts of resources."

Sid looks at me. I look back.

"Tell Shimon I said goodbye," I say.

"Sam—?" He stops. "No—this isn't right."

"It is, though," I say. "Tell the others I went home."

"No," says Sid, and he finally gets to his feet, and tries to get between me and the guys.

And Cooper knocks him down for a second time.

He doesn't say the *shma* this time.

"Enough," says Cooper. "Let's take whatever cash you old idiots have on hand, and what those housekeepers have on them too."

"Don't take their money!" I say. "They need it!"

Cooper grabs my ear. It's amazing how much that hurts.

"Shut up." He strokes my hair. "Such a pretty boy. You sure you're not a girl in there someplace?"

I force myself to look at him. I spit.

He slaps me.

I black out for a moment. And the next thing I know, I'm in the back seat of another fucking car that's heading back to Los Angeles.

My face hurts, and I have this intense stomach ache. Down below.

CHAPTER 22

Except we don't go there.

We go someplace else. To a tree lined street. Big houses. Cooper carries me into the house. The lights don't get turned on. He puts me in a room. He says, "sleep."

Unbelievably, I do sleep.

When I wake up, I feel funny. My pants feel wet. Have I wet my pants? I put my hand down my shorts. I pull it out. Red.

Oh great, I just got my first period.

I pull myself together and look around the room. And old-fashioned metal bed, with pretty pink and white sheets. A Kleenex box. I stuff some tissues into my pants. I look at the bed. I haven't stained anything. But my pants. I take them off and put them on the floor. I need—what do you call them—tampons. Or pads. I need to do laundry.

It would be nice if I had my meds. Dr. Gregorian said to take deep breaths for anxiety.

Breathe.

This room is clearly a girl's room—which seems ironic given all the gender non-conforming I've been working so hard at. I see bears and dolls lined up on shelves. The *Nancy Drew* books, and the *Narnia* books. Where is the girl who lives here? I walk over to the closet. Clothes. They look little though. I find a bathrobe—yellow terry. I put it on. It's too tight and too short, but I have to wear something. It barely closes. I look around for underwear. Tiny underpants. The girl is eleven, maybe ten.

Then I think of something.

I try the handle on the door.

It's not locked.

Voices outside my window.

I go to the frilly white lace curtains, and peek out, trying not to disturb the cloth.

The angelic drug dealer boy is talking to the guy named Cooper. Cooper lights a cigarette and walks away. The angelic boy goes back into the house—our house—I mean the house I'm in.

I sit on the floor for a second, holding the tissues up against me so I don't stain the bathrobe too.

Cooper scares me, but the other boy—I—could possibly deal with him.

Ha—no pun intended.

I look around the room.

Dr. Gregorian says a kid has to survive. That's the main thing.

My grandpa said he was lucky,

I hope I'm lucky too.

I don't see any scissors on the girl's desk. I look in the closet again. No nerf gun, no baseball bat. All old-fashioned girly stuff, it's why being a girl is so ridiculous. I wasn't crazy to want to be a boy.

And now this bleeding I mean I knew it was coming, but STILL. It's ridiculous.

It means I can have a baby.

A shudder goes through me when I think about Cooper. He seems like someone who could rape you. I'm just saying.

Then I wonder what that would feel like. Would it be horrible? I'm just wondering.

I hear shuffling around downstairs.

I need help, but I also need a weapon.

I see an umbrella in the corner next to a flouncy pink chair. A small one, but it's got a pointy end. It's an old-fashioned lady's umbrella. Full size not one of those dumb totes.

And I'm taller than the angel boy. And he's very skinny.

I pull the bathrobe around me. It gaps at the front of my hips.

I need pants. I rifle through the little drawers in the closet.

Tights. I finally find a footless pair, and jam them on me. They tear in the back, but I don't care I have to have something on my—my—ass, covering my—vagina, I guess I'd have to call it.

What will I ask for? What's my plan?

What do I have to offer?

I don't have time to figure it out. Cooper might come home and—whatever.

I open the door. I walk down the stairs. Nice ones. Old dark wood. I walk down to the main floor. Into a big, old-fashioned kitchen. This is such a nice place. Who lives here?

The angelic boy is drinking coffee and talking on the phone.

"I'm going to get it now," he says. "Should have it in an hour."

He sees me. Doesn't start. Which I take as a good sign.

Points at the coffee maker.

I guess today is the day I start drinking coffee. I pour myself a cup that I get out of the glass cabinet. Old fashioned. There's milk in a carton on the counter and I pour milk in the coffee like I've seen my mom do. The umbrella has a hook and it's around my wrist which looks fairly stupid, but I have to have something to brandish or poke a bad guy with, and I don't know where the knives are in the kitchen, and the angel boy is there looking at me.

I stand waiting for him to get off the phone.

"Well?" he says.

I stand there with my coffee and the umbrella and I guess I move or exhale or something, because my tights rip some more.

"Nice outfit, Sam," he says, "but I think it's a bit small."

Dr. Gregorian said that I am a good judge of character, and I should trust my gut instincts. "This doesn't mean doing something crazy," he said, "but I tend to think that if you listen to your gut, you'll be all right."

"I believe in you," he said to me once. That was my favorite session.

"You know my name," I say, sipping my coffee. It tastes terrible. "But I don't know yours."

"Dylan" he says. "Pleased to make your acquaintance, Sam."

He bows and I almost curtsey like they taught us at dancing school, but I stop, although wait—that's dumb—I'm going to have to tell him the truth in just a moment.

"Am I—can I?"

"Go?" he says. Of course. "Just don't tell the cops anything. If you do we'll deny it, and I've got connections, or rather my dad does."

They're really going to let me go? That seems crazy.

"It was just a scare tactic," he says. "I use them all the time with rich white people—they always get scared. They scare so easy."

Then I realize:

1. I have no clean clothes.

2. I don't have any money.

3. I don't know where I am.

4. I have no home to go to, because my parents are not interested, my grandmother is not interested, and my grandfather is the one who got me into this mess in the first place. Well, that's not fair. But it feels fair.

It strikes me that for the first time—ever—I'm really and truly alone and it totally sucks, just for your information. Rugged individualism is totally oversold; it's complete bullshit. Independence is only cool when you have people to be independent WITH and people to be independent FROM. But if you're all alone, you're just that.

So I do something I would never do under normal circumstances.

"Can I stay here for a while?" I ask Dylan.

And he says, "What's in it for me?"

I look at the kitchen sink. It's filled with dishes. I glance around. No dishwasher.

"I could help," I say.

Dylan lights a cigarette.

"I could like live here for a couple of weeks, 'til I sort things out," I say. "I could deliver messages for you, like the boy in *Oliver Twist*."

Dylan is playing with his phone, but he looks at me.

"Which one?"

"The Artful Dodger."

Dylan's lip curls. "So … you'd steal for me—so that makes me Fagin, and Cooper—he's the other one."

"Bill Sykes," I blurt out. Then I regret that, because Sykes is really a scary guy. I don't want him to be that guy.

On the other hand, am I really going to call my grandmother and tell her to come pick me up in—wherever the hell we are?

"By the way," I say. "Where are we?"

"Claremont," says Dylan.

"I was thinking more that I was Oliver…."

"Of course, you were," says Dylan. "You were thinking that you're a poor innocent little orphan who is going to be rescued by a sex worker who's going to return you to your rich guardian."

"Wait—I kind of AM an orphan."

"Not with those expensive Converses, you're not," says Dylan. He sits down but I stay standing up because I'm not sure what will happen to the tissue between my legs if I mess it up too much.

"Look" he says. "I'll take you to the library, and give you some money and you can make a phone call from the pay phone, and your mommy and daddy will come get you—we're not that far out of the city, and you can go and live your little early teen life with them and that will be the end of it."

I know this sounds crazy, but I don't want that offer.

"Listen, Dylan," I say. "First of all, my parents have gone missing. I don't know where they are."

I take a chance and sit down. The Kleenex jams up into me, which I think is probably a good sign. It's in the right place, more or less.

"Second of all, my grandmother sent me to a weird Torah camp which is kind of a wilderness place for Jewish kids, but the plumbing broke down and me and a few other kids ran away and ended up at the Old Age Home."

Dylan inhales and exhales. "Is this going to take much longer, or should I make myself some popcorn?"

"Third of all," I say. "I'm a girl, not a boy."

"And fourth, I just got my period, and I need clothes and some tampons."

Dylan puts out his cigarette and stands up. Picks up his cell phone. Makes a call.

"I'm going to be a few minutes late," he says to someone. "I have to go to Target."

"You should use pads rather than tampons," he says. "Your hymen may obstruct the tampon—presuming you still have a hymen."

I nod, my face getting hot.

"Thirteen," he says. "Right?"

He leaves. Comes back in a half an hour with a box of maxi-pads.

"Not sure about the size," he says.

Then. "You should probably come with me for the clothes.... but how can I trust you not to scream your head off, once we get in the store or anyplace public?"

I say, because it's the truth. "Because I don't have any place else to go."

He disappears and throws me an oversized t-shirt. I go upstairs, take off the bathrobe, and put on the t-shirt and situate the maxi-pad inside my ripped tights. I "think" the tights will hold through the shopping trip.

"OK.... Sam?" He picks up his keys again.

"Actually, it's Sarassine," I tell him.

"That's from a Balzac story," he says.

We drive to Target.

I get one dress on sale, and a package of underwear cheap.

"Get flip flops," he says. "They are useful."

I eye the tiny bras.

"Jesus," he says. "OK."

Then we go back to the house and I start in on the dishes.

CHAPTER 23

The first day is typical. I do the dishes. Doing dishes isn't hard. I've watched Olia do it, I've even helped her. Then I dry them. Before that, I go upstairs, and I take a shower. The bedroom that I am in has its own bathroom, or rather it shares with another room that no one sleeps in. But still, I lock both doors, and I get cleaned up and I put on my dress and my underpants and my pad. I put my other pants in the sink in cold water. To soak the blood out. There is an old stick of deodorant in the medicine cabinet. I use it. There is an old bottle of shampoo in the shower. I make do. It isn't ideal. But it is cool in a way to be in this almost empty space, with nothing of my parents and nothing from my past and nothing that is mine in it.

My backpack sits empty of cash on the girl's desk.

I come out of the bathroom, and I comb my hair with my fingers. The bangs are getting long. I find a child's barrette and I put it through the bangs, sweeping them to the side. I look at myself in the mirror. I'm not sure who it is that I see in there. But for a moment— just a moment—I like who I see.

I do the dishes—like I just said—and then I look around for a broom, and I sweep the kitchen floor—like I saw Rusty do at camp. I walk around the room that I guess is the living room. I empty out the ashtrays.

Dylan is on the phone a lot. Then he goes out.

I am alone in the house. I think about Cooper coming back, but I don't think he will, and so I stop being afraid of *that* for a while.

I open the refrigerator. I find peanut butter and jelly and an open bag of sliced bread.

I make three sandwiches.

I eat them.

That first day, I look around for a landline telephone, but there isn't one. There is a TV but no cable. I flick it on and then off.

The first few days, I stay inside all day. I scrounge the cabinets for food. I watch for Cooper. But it gets hot inside the house, which doesn't seem to have any air-conditioning. So, the fifth day, I go inside a room that is like a den. It has lots of old books. Through French doors, I see a backyard with big trees. I choose a book at random and go outside. There are some old broken lawn chairs. I go back inside and get a towel. I arrange the towel on the grass and lie down with the book, but I don't open it.

I look around. On one side is a church, with occasional people going in and out. And on the other side is a house that looks like this one.

It's nice to be quiet and alone with just my thoughts. I think about all kinds of stuff. I wonder what Jackie is doing, and I think about alternate endings for *Pan's Labyrinth* and for *Twelfth Night*. Does *The Shape of Water* really have to have so much sex in it at the very beginning? Did Shimon go back through time, or did he go back to being dead, and if the former rather than the latter, did he bring Victor with him, even though you're not supposed to time-travel? What would I say to Rusty if he were to show up right now? How is Hannah and does she have a job as an assistant lifeguard? Does she think about me?

I sleep, I guess. It's been a tiring summer.

"Your legs are going to get sunburned," someone calls to me.

I jump a little, because I hear that male voice and I think of Cooper, but it's an older voice, so I don't completely freak. I sit up and look and it's a man in the yard next door, calling through the fence.

"Oh," I said. Thanks."

"Are you a relative?" the guy says. I look at him and yeah he is older—not OLD like my dad, but older than Dylan and Cooper.

"Yes," I say. "I'm visiting my cousins."

"Well, enjoy Claremont," he says. Then he pauses. "I sure hope your—cousins—spend some time showing you around—they are out a lot."

"OK," I say. "Thanks—"

"Peter," he says. "I'm Peter, and you are?"

"Sarassine," I say.

"Wow," he says leaning on the fence. "That's an unusual name. Sarassine what?"

I try to think of something, and then I realize that I don't know what Dylan's last name is so it's going to be a bit weird making the familial connection.

For some reason when I think of lying I always think of my grandpa. He used to make up crazy stories about the family and told them to me when I was visiting and had trouble falling asleep. "Grandma was once a tightrope walker in the circus," he told me, "And she tried to teach your father tightrope walking, but he was afraid of heights, so he went into the law." Apparently, he told pretend stories all the time in Germany to keep him and his preschool friends amused and later he told stories so people wouldn't feel sorry for him. Pretend stories also keep people kind of off-balance. So, they can't hurt you.

"Frankfurt," I say. And then I remember something my babysitter said. "If grownups ask you for information, be sure to ask for information back."

"And you?" I say.

"McCarthy," he says. "Frankfurt, like the city?" he says. "Is that German?"

"It is," I say. "It means 'city of hot dogs.'"

"Nice talking to you," says Peter McCarthy. "I have to go to work now."

"I need to go inside now anyway," I say. Then I go in the backdoor, lock it, and check the front door too. I look out the side-windows as Peter McCarthy walks past but doesn't get into a van in his driveway.

McCarthy Plumbing it says on the side.

At last, I think, *a real plumber.*

CHAPTER 24

As I look out the window, I see Dylan parking his car and getting out. He's got Cooper with him. I go upstairs and go into "my" bedroom. I put the desk chair under the doorknob of the main door, and I lock the other side of the bathroom door. I just don't want to be surprised.

I hear them talking downstairs in the kitchen, but I can't make out what they're saying. So I figure I've got to get proactive. I let myself out and walk nearer to the head of the stairs.

"Dylan—the rest of the money just got wired from the old people," says Cooper.

Dylan responds with something inaudible.

"So, drive that girl to the Metrolink station and put her on the train to LA. We're like kidnappers of a minor or something."

Dylan says something back to him, but I still can't hear it. I tiptoe out of my room, because the floorboards creak.

"You're out of your—" says Cooper. "Fuck it, I'm going to stay with Regina."

I duck behind the railing as Cooper goes to the front door.

"But I need you to drive me," he says.

Dylan comes to the front of the house.

"I've never fucking heard of a dealer who doesn't know how to drive."

"I'm a sculptor," says Cooper. "We live on a higher—." The door slams.

It gets dark. It's funny but when you're alone in a house in the day-time it's kind of cool and fun, but when you're alone in a house in the dark and the guys you are living with are drug dealers who you don't know at all, the situation feels very different.

I sit in the living room and look out the window.

The streetlights come on, and I see a shadow glide over the side-walk.

"Shimon?" I say.

Silence.

The shadow slides up the steps and slips through the crack in the front door.

It's here. With me. In the house. It rears up very large on the entranceway hall.

I run through the kitchen out into the backyard. There's a gate that links "our" backyard with an alley. I run out into it.

I run smack into the plumber from next door.

"What the—"

"I got scared," I say.

"Come into my house," he says, and he holds out his hand.

He seems quite nice.

But he's much bigger than Dylan. And older. And while I'm just a kid, who's just become—technically—a woman, even I know that going into the domicile of a strange male adult is kind of risky.

And I hate to admit this, but the fact that I'm White and he's Black makes me a little afraid of him. I don't know any Black adult men, I'm realizing.

"Never mind," I say. I run back into the house.

The Shadow is still there in the front hall.

I grab my little girl's umbrella from the umbrella stand and point it. I can't think of what else to do, so I just yell out that silly magic word that actually seems to have some power to it.

"*Abracadabra!*" I shout.

A figure falls at my feet.

A white guy with long hair.

"Who are you?" I say.

He says, "The writer." Only he doesn't *say* it, exactly. He writes it in the air with his finger. The words hover in white, like an Instagram thing you put on your story, and then the letters drip and disappear.

"Are you alive?" I say.

"*No*," he says/writes.

There's a knock on the front door.

"Can you protect me?" I say.

"*Sometimes.*"

"Can you protect me now?"

"*I think so,*" is the answer.

I look through the side windows of the front door.

It's Peter the plumber again.

"Are you OK?" he shouts.

"I'm OK," I shout back.

I look at the man with the long hair. He nods at me.

"Sorry—Dylan, my uh cousin told me—not to open the door at night."

The writer stands between me and the door, which is not terribly helpful because I can see the door right through his semi-transparent midsection. He writes something in his hand, then lifts his palm and blows the contents through the hinges—I guess that's how he got in in the first place.

I see the letters SHE IS FINE sail through and emerge on the other side.

There is a pause.

"OK," says Peter. "Have a good night."

He goes away, but he does look back at the house a couple of times.

The writer sits in the den. He produces a pen and what looks like a yellow legal pad out of thin air.

He writes. Furiously.

I sit with him and read the book that I pulled from the shelf in "my" room. It's a kid's book called *The Deserted Village*.

We sit together until Dylan comes home.

CHAPTER 25

The next morning it is snowing.

I sit up in bed in the girl's room that might have been mine but isn't and look out the window and see the flakes falling down on the backyard. I put on my dress, and my Converse trainers, but it is so cold I have to cover myself with a blanket—I guess they call it a "throw"—that is lying on the bed.

I go downstairs.

Dylan is not in the kitchen, but on the kitchen table there's a little glass—I guess they call it a shot glass—sitting in front of a lit candle. Next to that is a photograph in a silver frame, surrounded by flowers. Folded over the chair is a fur coat.

The photograph is a picture of a blonde woman in a white halter dress. She looks a little like Marilyn Monroe. Red lipstick, gold earrings. And with her is a little boy.

You look at the eyes and the way the boy stands and the way his very blonde hair curls over his forehead, make it so you can see right away it is Dylan. He smiles shyly at the camera.

It's always so weird to realize that everybody—I mean EVERY-BODY—was a little kid once. Had a mother once. Even Stalin. Even Hitler. Even Trump.

Even Grandma.

Someday I will look at myself as I was in a picture. And I'll think *was I ever that little?* I hope I can remember that yes, once upon a time, I was. And then one day I was older, and one day—like today—I was both big and small, "right smack dab," as my grandpa would say between the stages, and could look both forward and backward, and see my entire life, a ribbon extending in back and in front of me in time.

That's maybe why adolescence is so weird. You can see all the possibilities and all the roads. And yet, you're in a singular timeline, and you can't control any of it.

Anyway.

So why is it snowing in Southern California in the summertime?

I go back upstairs and start moving quietly down the old-fashioned hallway. Spacious, with a window seat looking out over the backyard.

Dylan is sitting on it.

He is smoking a joint.

I hardly make a sound.

But he hears me.

"It always snows on her *yahrzeit*," he says to me, inhaling on the joint.

"I'm freezing," I say.

"Yes," he says. "Death is cold."

He turns towards me, and I see that his eyes are really big.

I'm about to ask him what he's on, but he stands up and holds out his hand.

It keeps on surprising me how young-looking Dylan is. Like he ought to be my age. He's like a Jewish angel crossed with Peter Pan. His eyes are really blue.

"Come on," he says. He takes my

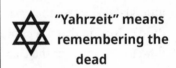 **"Yahrzeit" means remembering the dead**

This is Yiddish (again) and the word literally means "time of year." Jewish people light a special candle every year on the anniversary of the death of a family member and they go to synagogue and say a special prayer known as **"kaddish."** I think you can also have people come to your house and say it with you (you need a minyan—aka 10 people [remember?]) but I'm not sure. I really like that we get to feel sad about the death of the people we love, no matter how long ago it was. See https://en.wikipedia.org/wiki/Yahrzeit_candle

hand. His own hand is cold and thin—like a frozen piece of paper. His skin, though, is smooth.

Maybe it's because he's shorter than me and looks so young that I'm not afraid of Dylan, although I know you're going to tell me I should be, and what the hell was the weird scene at the old age camp.... Maybe it isn't all in front of us who people are.... Maybe.... I don't know.

I glance in the den as we walk to the front door.

The writer is not there.

I look outside. Icicles drip from the roof of the old porch.

"Don't we need coats?" I say.

Dylan shakes his head. "It won't help. And there's no point in calling attention to ourselves."

We walk out. The writer is waiting for us outside. He's wearing a plain short sleeved shirt, Bermuda shorts, and snowshoes.

Dylan cocks his head. "Hi," he says to him in a way that makes me think he knows who the writer is. And then, "Your long hair is stupid, dude."

The writer looks at Dylan, whips out his yellow pad from someplace, and writes feverishly.

We look across the street at some workmen fixing something.

They have hard hats on and even from here I can see that they are all sweating.

"Man, this heat," says one of them.

I stick out my tongue to catch a snowflake.

"See?" says Dylan.

We scrape the ice off the car, with a scraper.

The workmen look over at us for a second. Then they turn away.

We get in the car.

The writer hops on top of the car trunk. I can see the back of him.

"Why is he coming with us?" I say.

"To nag me and anyone else around here who thinks they want to be a writer to 'keep to their writing practice and not give up,'" says Dylan. "I thought about being a writer once. I wanted to be a writer like *him*."

"Why am *I* seeing him?" I say.

"Were you paying attention to what I just said?"

We drive to the post office.

"Wait for me. This will just take a few minutes," says Dylan.

"No," I say. "I want to come in too." I jerk my head to the back where the writer is still perched.

"Not a good idea," says Dylan. He points at a building across the street. "How about the library? Go improve your mind or something for ten minutes."

I walk into the library. It goes from cold to hot in about one second.

The writer walks in with me too. But first he takes off his snowshoes and puts them by the side of the door, as though they were umbrellas.

I haven't been in a library other than the Hancock Park library in a long time. Anyway, it's interesting how there is still a lot of paper in the library. Pamphlets and flyers. Announcements. It's cool how much paper there is here, as though hard copies still mattered.

I don't know what to do so I look around.

Down the hall, there are two orange pylons with a handwritten piece of paper taped to them that reads:

```
we apologize for the inconvenience—RESTROOMS
                 out of order
```

I raise my eyebrows to myself. Nod.

I wonder what Tomy and Sofia are doing?

What's happening to my house?

Where are my parents?

I look at the corkboard where a lot of stuff is being announced in an old-timey way.

Book clubs

Veteran's book club

Seniors book club

Children's reading.

TEEN VOLUNTEERS NEEDED

I look over at the writer. He is bending over someone who is reading at a big table. He looks up at me. He smiles.

He seems happier here with the books.

I go over to the information desk.

There's a regulation library lady there, with her long dress and her pearls and her hair in a kind of no-nonsense short style, and glasses.

She, too, smiles a nice smile, when I go up to her.

I feel like it's been a long time since any adult really smiled at me.

I say, "I would like to volunteer."

Then I think *shit!* because I realize I should worry about identification and the fingerprints and the *Minority Report* movie retinal display—I'm kidding about that, but you know what I mean—but I guess the library is so unimportant now, so off the grid, so what my mom would call "marginalized"—that the librarian woman asks for my address and phone number, and I give them the LA ones, but explain that I'm spending the summer with my cousin, and he lives right up the street.

The lady says "OK, well please get the local contact information to us," and she gives me a form to take home and have a parent or guardian sign.

I think *uh oh,* but then she says, "We are so happy to have young people help. Big kids help little kids understand how important reading is, so if you like, I'll put you to work right now."

I feel like I better go tell Dylan what is happening, so I excuse my-self, saying "Great—let me tell my cousin," and the librarian woman whose nameplate reads "Eun-Jee" says "that's fine," in her quiet but firm library voice, and as I walk out, I hold my index finger up at the writer, which means "wait," and run across the street to the Post Office.

Dylan is standing in a huge line.

"Get the hell out," he says very softly, looking at a cop who has just appeared by the door.

"I'm volunteering at the library." I say.

"Who cares?" he says. "Go. I'll find you later."

It has stopped snowing over the roof of Dylan's car. The snow is crystalizing, melting on the roof.

I walk back into the library.

Eun-Jee puts me to work, showing books to and reading out loud to little kids in the children's part of the library.

"What's your name?" one tiny child with black hair asks.

"Viola" I say.

"Like violin?" says a kid.

"Like the hero in a play by Shakespeare," I say. "A play about a shipwreck—a play about a girl who is a survivor."

"What's a survivor?" asks another kid.

"Someone who lives."

A third kid nods. "We know all about that," she says, and she pulls out a book called *My Papi Has a Motorcycle*. And I read it to the three of them right there in the stacks.

I work at the library for the entire day, which I was not expecting but it works out fine, mostly, until the end. Eun-Jee goes and gets me a sandwich since it's my first day and I don't have any money. I eat in the staff break room, which is cool and grown-up feeling. I'm staff! (Kind of [not really, but still it feels cool]). Then I learn about shelving the kids' stuff. Then I read some more books out loud.

I leave the building a couple of times to go across the street to the deli whose bathroom is working (they haven't felt my presence yet, I think to myself).

This is a pretty cool downtown. They even have a shoe repair store. I go in. I take out my red Gucci bat mitzvah slingbacks. The man says he can fix the broken heel, but I'll have to leave them.

I do. He gives me a ticket. I don't know if I'll ever get the money to pay for them, but it doesn't matter....

I'm feeling ... almost ... happy.

I notice that Dylan's car is not on the street anymore.

I don't worry about that. Life is short and he's probably running errands. I find a paper map of downtown Claremont at the city hall building. Just there in one of those see-through plastic display pockets. For free. And I find the street where Dylan's house is.

Sixth Street is not far. I figure I could even walk there if I needed to.

I like the library. I like the kids. And the feeling of learning and being alone together with people. I like going on the computers, and googling things. I stay at one computer, and then go to the next and then the next, 'til I've googled something on the whole line of them.

Menstruation

Sexual orientation

Gender identity/fluidity

Synagogues of Claremont

High schools in Claremont

California Drug Law

Dresses or Pants?

Queer Shakespeare

The writer seems to be settling in as well. He is currently sitting at the last computer, and he is tapping on the keyboard.

He sees me coming and puts his arms over the screen.

"Why is what you're writing a secret?" I ask him. He puts his fingers to his lips.

I whisper the question.

"*It's my suicide note,*" he scribbles in the air with one of those little pencils they have sometimes at the library. The penciled words hang in the air for a moment, and an elderly woman who has imperfectly hidden her chihuahua in her purse (its head is sticking out), glimpses it before she walks through the words, and they drip down her shoulders while the semi-concealed dog goes yap.

"Did you kill yourself?" I don't know why but that interests me. It's such a radical thing to do and it must hurt and it's well kind of un-take-backable.

Someone comes and sits on the writer. Or rather through him. And uses the computer.

I go back to reading for some kids, as a new batch of them seem to arrive every hour. I pick *Frog and Toad Are Friends*. One of my favorites. It makes me think of Jackie. How we used to fight over who was Toad, because he was the really cranky one and we loved him yelling at the flowers. And we loved them celebrating Christmas together.

Then it starts to get late. The kids go home and I'm sitting there, and I've used the bathroom a bunch of times at the deli and now the deli is closed.

Eun-Jee looks at me.

"Is there someone I should call?" she says.

"My cousin," I say. "He must be running late."

I watch the sun set, and the dark comes. But it's light in the library. They are open late, which is nice, and people are coming in to look things up, and then come to a book club, and then borrow CDs and it's pretty busy.

I listen idly to the book club leader.

"*The Odyssey* is considered by many to be a novel, although it's of course an epic, which means a narrative told in verse."

"Odysseus tries to come home, but he is blocked by the gods, while his wife the faithful Penelope waits. In the meantime, Telemachus, his son, tries to protect the kingdom."

The son again, I think. *What about the daughter who tries to protect the kingdom? And what about a kingdom where the toilets don't work, and the pipes are broken, and everything is jutting up through the floor, and no one is in charge to supervise the repairs…. What about a home where no one lives? What about a daughter no one thinks about?*

Where's that frigging epic? I think.

The book club has all turned to me and I realize that everything I've just thought to myself, I've just said out loud.

"That's a good question," says the woman with the chihuahua hidden in her purse. "What about epics starring women and girls?"

"Well," says a younger woman in the group. "There's Buffy, and before that there's Sarah Connor."

The letters spelling out "*Circumscribed lives under patriarchy*" swim up from the ground. The writer is lying on the floor smoking a pipe and the words smoke out of the barrel.

"The lives of women in Homer's civilization were quite circumscribed," says the book club leader.

"By patriarchy," I say. "Yeah, I know. So how about reading the novel *Circe* instead?"

I walk over to the counter where Eun-Jee is.

"I'm going to go outside and wait for my cousin," I tell her.

She looks at me. "Come back in, if he doesn't show up." She takes a piece of paper and one of the little pencils.

"You can call this number if you need anything." Above the number she has printed *Hostel for homeless teens.*

I wonder a little if Eun-Jee suspects something, but she gives me the paper and goes back to organizing whatever it is she's organizing on her librarian desk.

"Bye," I tell her.

"Be well," she says.

I go sit on the steps. The writer comes out after me.

"Why did you kill yourself?" I ask him.

He blows smoke letters that say, "*I don't know.*"

We look out at the street.

It's a clear night—which is unusual for California—and the streetlights have come on. Kids are skateboarding up and down the sidewalks. There's a girl with bright green hair in a bikini top and a mini skirt who, if Jackie were here, would say she was doing basic stuff, like ollies and kickflips, but she's making them look good. Then she goes over to a bench and sips on a drink with a boy and a girl. The two others sit very still, while she runs her board back and forth with her foot. The wheels make a growling sound.

"How can you not know why you killed yourself?" I say to the writer.

"*Because, it was chemical,*" he says/writes.

I think about my meds.

"Will I do that, or will it happen to me?"

The writer looks at me. He is or was very handsome. I bet he was famous. He kind of has that quality to him.

"*No,*" he says/writes.

"How can you tell for sure?"

At that moment, Dylan pulls up.

I'm kind of mad that he's been gone for hours but the fact is I've also had a good day, the best day I've had in years, it feels like.

That's when I remember. Because seriously things have been so weird, and there has been so much midsummer madness, to quote *Twelfth Night,* that I haven't really thought about it at all.

Today is my birthday. I'm officially fourteen.

And sitting in his car, Dylan looks like a Renaissance angel. Blonde curls and blue eyes. He's skinny, but in a cute way.

I don't know what to say, so I don't say anything.

He doesn't say he's sorry. He just reaches over and opens the passenger door.

The writer gets on the roof and lies down.

I get in. We drive "home"—the closest thing to home I've had in some time. I wonder if I'll ever go home again. I wonder if I care. I mean in *Romeo and Juliet* people get married at thirteen. I mean, couldn't I just like stay here? Volunteer at the library? Go to high school here?

It's an old house, like the ones you see on old TV sitcoms or in old movies. "Craftsman," I think you call it. My mom loves these houses.

CHAPTER 26

"Listen—" Dylan says as we get out of the car. "I need to tell you a story."

The writer stays on the front porch in the darkness, while we go inside. Dylan lights a joint in the old fashioned kitchen. I take off my backpack and sit at the table and smoke with him. He explains why he was so late and why he left me all alone at the library today.

As he starts telling, the snow starts falling again outside our window. It doesn't get cold again though, maybe because I'm listening. I try to listen as hard as I can: to pour all my listening into a fire, not a Kabbalistic fire, but my own fire, made up of all the things I am that maybe won't call forth any spirits, but that will be all attention.

But that's easier said than done particularly if you're exhausted from a kind of intense day, and things are bothering you that you don't have words for, and you've been off your dyspraxia meds for a couple of months now. And tbh, Dylan's story is long and technical, and so I can't focus on all of it.

But here's the gist. There's apparently a mix-up with a package at the post office, which is why he tells me to get the hell out of there, when I come to the post office to find him. The original package has drugs in it, and it goes missing and Dylan and Cooper have to find a replacement, and then try to figure out what happened—which they don't. There's a lot of driving around, trying not to look suspicious in front of the cop at the post office, and then delivering replacement drugs to a rock band who are having a party/concert at a loft in Pomona, and the whole thing has been a big bummer, because all Dylan wanted to do was sit at home today and drop acid.

I ask why.

"Sarassine," he says. "Because that's what I **always** do. I do a whole ritual for my mom with eating and drinking, and then I drive to the cemetery near Disney Headquarters and visit her grave. And drop some more acid. But it's too late to go to the cemetery now."

I look at the *yahrzeit* candle burning in its little glass.

"Let's do the rest of the ritual right now," I say.

Dylan looks at me. He raises an eyebrow. Then he rearranges the picture of the beautiful woman who looks like Marilyn Monroe—his mother—so it's further from the *yahrzeit* candle and closer to the lilies and the orchids on the table. He goes to the refrigerator and gets out a carton of pate and a box of crackers. He sets those on the table along with tiny, fancy china cocktail plates.

Then he goes to a cupboard and gets out a bottle of whiskey. He pours out two glasses.

I hate whiskey. But I lift my glass and toast. I sip the burning liquid.

I open my mouth to ask, but Dylan sees it coming

"She died out in the Hamptons of a drug overdose. I was fifteen."

I try to speak again, but he cuts me off.

"Whatever. Everyone has something to bring to the tragedy table."

I munch on a few crackers. Eat some pate, which is really good. Dylan takes a few shots. He gets out some tablets which I presume are acid, and is about to swallow them when his cell phone rings.

"I—can't," he says. "I'll deal with that later."

He drinks again and looks at me.

"My mom drank whiskey and dropped acid too, although, what she really loved was doing coke and shopping for outerwear."

He stands up.

"I'll show you. Upstairs. Hall closet." He takes my hand and we walk up the stairs. He opens a closet door. The closet is full of coats and jackets: leather, and cloth, and faux fur. An array of brilliant colors that remind me somehow of the colors I saw emanating from the *sefirot* design on the floor of the B'nai Ahava senior home.

I can't help myself; I stroke the fuzzy wool of a bright purple jacket.

"Yeah, I do exactly what you are doing," he says. "I stroke them like you just did."

Dylan leans against the closet door.

"She was amazing, and smart, and too much for my father. Drugs killed her technically, but I think more it was her life—that fucking bourgeois upper class bullshit of empty conversations and meaning-less sports activities. I just hope I wasn't part of that—the part of her life that was too little for her because it was everything that she didn't want."

"Are you an only child?" I ask.

"No," Dylan answers. "I'm the eldest. There is me, my sister— you're in her room—and my two little brothers. This house was a vacation home from when we still lived in NYC. Claremont, the city of trees and PhD's. My mom liked going to all the lectures on the seven campuses. She wanted to go to grad school, but never did."

"So if she died in the Hamptons, why is she buried in LA and not in New York?"

"Because, dummy, it's where we all moved. Remember? My dad thought if she got away from the East Coast, she'd calm down somehow." He laughs "As if Los Angeles calmed anybody down. She made new connections. New lovers. New friends, and new dealers. Then she just flew back and forth between parties, lovers, and dealers on both coasts. And then she OD'd."

He runs his fingers over a brilliantly yellow coat.

"Anyway, Sarassine, I'm sorry I left you alone at the library."

I stand in the hallway with the closet door open, listening to Dylan's story. Stroking his dead mother's coats.

Dylan is something I've never seen before. A genuinely tragic person. I guess, kind of like my grandfather who escaped Hitler thanks to the pretend plumber, but his older brother—who was already studying engineering with their uncle and aunt in San Diego—died of TB. So, weirdly, my grandfather survived, but his older brother didn't.

And, come to think of it, my grandfather didn't have his mother either. His mother died in Germany, before he left. She died of cancer. And his father had died long before.

So, Hans Anfang grew up with his uncle and his aunt. But he didn't have any immediate family. Until he got married, that is.

Something starts to happen to me.

First off, I start to forgive Grandpa a little. I think I understand— a bit—why he felt such a—loyalty, I guess you'd say—to angry, Zumba-exercising, obsessively sock-folding, Godiva-Chocolate-eating, kabbalah-practicing Grandma.

Then another feeling starts to happen. A big feeling.

I guess sometimes you suddenly feel so much for a person that you're about to burst with it. That's what's happening to me. For Dylan. Who is angry but also scared. Who is an entry-level genius, but who is also in pain. Who is bad in some ways. But who is also good and even sweet, because he is loyal to the people he loves, even though they sound like they are—or were—pretty fucked up. Aka his mom.

Loyalty is a good thing. Remembrance is a good thing. Jackie has always been loyal to me and it's one of the reasons that I love them and will never forget them. Sid was loyal too. I know some loyal people.

And … despite their many flaws, my parents … are not horrible people. They aren't drug addicts who fly from party to party. And they aren't dead (as far as I know).

There's something else too. Dylan is the first person I have dealt with this whole wack summer who has actually had the courage to apologize and—I think—mean it.

So I kiss him.

He tastes like booze and he tastes like sadness and kind of a grownup-too-fast boy.

I pull back for instant and explain the only way I can think to.

"Today's my birthday," I tell him. "I'm fourteen."

Now he kisses me back. He puts his arms around me and now we are skinny Jewish kid to skinny Jewish kid. Genius drug dealer to average intelligence neurodivergent teenaged life-saving student who does have a talent for empathy. Short orphan to tall run away.

Our hips bump against each other and click into place. My dress against his t-shirt. I can feel his chest against mine. It's so strange. For someone who makes it snow, his body is really hot. His heart pounds. Or perhaps it's mine.

We squeeze tighter. We keep on kissing.

That's when the cops come.

They actually say what they say in those classic original *Perry Mason* TV shows that my dad loves: "Open up. This is the police."

CHAPTER 27

"Do you have a warrant?" Dylan takes his mouth away from mine to shout back, loudly and naturally, as though he's done it before.

Then he whispers the words he's said before, but he does it kindly, softly.

"Go," he says. Then he kisses me once more. Very lightly.

I run down the stairs, grab my backpack, and dash out the backdoor into the backyard, which the cops haven't entered yet. I go through the fence.

I walk into the alley.

And run straight into Cooper.

"Cooper," I say. "The COPS!"

"What did you do!" he grabs me. "This is your fault," he says. "Come with me."

Not this time, I think, and I do something unoriginal. I kick him in the shins and run past him down the alley towards the church.

I see a set of stairs going down.

I go down them.

Actually, I fall down them. Dyspraxia in action.

It's only four steps. So I don't break anything.

But I'm a little disoriented so when I hear a voice say softly "What the fuck!" I don't stand up right away. I stay on my hands and knees and look around.

There are a few bare light bulbs running down the side of a concrete wall. There's a station wagon parked with a cross on the driver's door. The words **Church Carpool** are printed in white block letters on the floor of the parking space.

"What the fuck do you want?" says that same voice again. I stand up and turn away from the stairs.

Almost right in back of me, with her back against the wall—literally—is the girl with the green hair who I saw outside the library. She's holding her skateboard up high like she's going to beat me over the head with it.

"Don't hit me!" I say. I put my hand up. I try to catch my breath. "I'm just hiding here for a minute."

"Get out," says the girl with the green hair.

"Just give me a minute," I say. I look at her and inhale.... exhale. That's when I notice that the two kids who were with her earlier on the bench outside—a girl and a boy—are there too, standing behind her. Alert. Ready to.... What?

"Look," I say. "I just need a few minutes 'til the cops are g—."

"GET. OUT. NOW," hisses the girl with the green hair. "Or I'll—"

"Wait," says the second girl. The boy tenses, but she puts her hand on his shoulder. She walks in front of the green hair girl.

She looks at me. She squints her eyes, studying my face.

"I know you," she says. "Sam?"

I look back at her. She's beautiful. She has long black hair that she has tucked behind her ears.

"How—" I start. And then I stop.

My mom always says that despite the freeways and the sprawl, SoCal is just a really spread out, very poorly designed small town, and that's why you just keep running into the same people over and over again, like the way she cannot seem to avoid seeing German collagists, even when she tries to escape the city and goes out as far as the Mall at Moreno Valley or goes to refresh her spirits at the dinosaur park in Jurupa, because LA gets her down sometimes she says with its obsession with fame and money.

"Yes," I say. "How.... Why.... did you guys leave Baruch Bardot?"

Green Hair lowers her board, and the boy steps forward.

"ICE," he says.

"What's that?" I say.

"Immigration and Customs Enforcement," says Green Hair. "ICE came for them after the camp closed. Picked up the parents and most of the kids."

"But not me and Esteban," says the girl with the long black hair who I saw a million years ago helping her—I guess—parents and her—I guess—brother with the gardening at that first long ago Jewish summer camp.

"How do you know my name?" I say.

"She listens and watches," says Esteban.

"What's YOUR name?

"Estrella." Estrella turns to Green Hair.

"And this is Tiffany—we met her hitchhiking."

Tiffany salutes in a semi-sarcastic way.

"And what are YOU doing here?" says Tiffany.

"Long story," I say. "Can I go where you're going?"

"We don't have a place right now," says Tiffany. "And we're out of cash. Got any money?"

"No," I say. "What will you do?"

"We were trying to figure that out, when you fell down on us," Tiffany says.

I rummage in my backpack and find the piece of paper Eun-Jee gave me. "What about the youth shelter?"

"*They* can't go there!" Tiffany says. "They need a lawyer or something. And I don't need a stupid shelter. I've been on my own for two years."

I am having the beginning of an idea, but Tiffany interrupts again.

"You better leave. The cops may be looking for you." And to the others, "We need to keep moving."

"Hang out here for a bit," I say. "I might be able to ask someone to help."

Esteban sits on the concrete.

"I'm tired," he says. Tiffany sits down next to him.

"I know," she says. Then she starts talking to him about someone she knows in Upland and how she thinks they can maybe crash with them.

I am about to put my backpack back on my shoulders, but Estrella stops me.

"Wait," she says. "Here—"

She hands me a beaded necklace. It has a cross on the end.

"My mom gave me this before we left El Salvador," Estrella says. "She didn't make it across. But she said 'take it so whatever happens you don't forget me.' Take it now, so you don't forget us."

I don't want to take Estrella's necklace, but she holds her arm out in that strong way that people have when you know they won't take no for an answer.

I hold my hand out and the beads click together into my palm. I stow the necklace in my pack so I don't lose it.

I think for a second. Then I unclasp the barrette that I've been wearing to hold back my bangs—the one I took from Dylan's sister's bedroom.

I give the barrette to Estrella. She smiles and puts it in her hair.

"Now we are friends," she says. "Because we have exchanged gifts."

"For fuck's sake," says Tiffany.

"OK—I'm going," I say back.

Estrella leans over and whispers in my ear, "I will convince her to stay here. It's not bad, and we're next to the church, and we can run in there, if we have to."

"Your English is so good!" I whisper back.

"One year in Simi Valley High School," she whispers. "Also—I like you this way ... dressed like a girl."

I walk back up the stairs.

I think about the people I barely noticed at Baruch Bardot. The gardeners and the cooks. Those kids, who were so good at avoiding us, disappearing in a second when we came along. They must have been afraid we would turn them in. That's what the Germans did, when the Nazis searched the cities and countryside for Jews in hiding. So many Germans just went along with the government.

Collaborated.

Remember this. Remember this. Remember this.

CHAPTER 28

I walk back into the alley.

No sign of Cooper.

But just to be on the safe side, I run into the plumber's backyard. I hang out in their garden shed for a few minutes. I'm tired of running and hiding, but when you are a teenager who is not eighteen, your life is circumscribed by patriarchy, which means—in this instance—adults. Adultocracy. I decide at this point that I'm going to have to go home.

I wait until the police cars leave. Dylan continues to yell at them that he needs to see a warrant, which they don't have. There's more back and forth yelling, and eventually the cops go away, even as they threaten in no uncertain terms to come back. I walk through the side yard to the front of the plumber's house, and I just think *what the fuck* and I ring the doorbell.

I hesitate for a moment.

Before I push the doorbell, I remember something I haven't thought about in a long time. A couple of summers ago, I was over at Jackie's house, and we were reading books from the library, when they took their copy of *The Hunger Games* and hurled it across the room so hard, it knocked over the potted palm in their living room. The pot fell over and smashed and dirt spilled all over the marble floor.

"What's the matter?" I said.

"I hate this book," they said.

I mean the HUNGER GAMES is not everyone's favorite, but I remember I was kind of scared by the reaction. It was so unlike Jackie to get that angry. I walked over to them and put my hand on their shoulder. They jerked their shoulder away, so all I could do was stand there next to them, as they glared out between the expensive window treatments. A couple of minutes went by.

"If one more Black person dies …" they said. "Just to keep the fucking story moving."

I looked at their face, as two tears trickled down—one on each cheek.

"I'm sorry," was all I could think of to say.

I ring the bell.

Peter answers the door.

"Are you OK?" he says.

"I'm fine," I say, "but I need to use your phone."

He gestures and I walk in.

A white woman with red hair is sitting and reading.

"Hi," she says.

I say hi back.

"I'm sorry if I scared you earlier," he says to me. "Reagan tells me I scare people, because I'm so tall."

"And Black," Reagan adds. "After all, this is Claremont."

"No problem," I say. "And to be honest … I … was kind of a racist back there."

I do what my mom always does with the German collagists after there's been a misunderstanding.

I stick out my hand. "I.… I apologize."

He shakes my hand.

I appreciate that the two of them don't ask me any questions about why I'm here, and what the cops are doing next door.

Who knows? They may have secrets too that they don't want to reveal.

Everyone has something to bring to the tragedy table.

Reagan points me to an actual landline phone.

I call my father's cell, and then my mother's.

I think I knew they weren't going to answer, but I had to give them a try before taking a deep breath and tapping the numbers into my grandmother's cell phone.

She answers the phone with her usual holler.

"Stop calling me. I no longer support the Conservatives for Israeli Dominance," she shouts.

"Grandma," I say. "It's me, Sarassine. I'm in Claremont. I need help to come home."

To her credit, she doesn't scream. Or hang up.

She calmly says, "OK, what is the address?" and she sends a car service. She doesn't like Uber.

"They mistreat the drivers and it's a *shande*," she says.

While I wait for the car to come, I figure I should take this opportunity to finally talk to a real plumber about plumbing.

I just launch in.

"So—I want to be a plumber. How did **you** get started?" I ask Peter.

> ### ❓ How's your Yiddish?
>
> "**Shande**" is the Yiddish word for "shame." In context it means something is disgraceful, unacceptable, and morally wrong, like preventing workers in the gig-economy from unionizing, as Zack pointed out to me.

He looks at me strangely, and I point at the van parked outside.

"No," he says. "I'm a pre-school teacher."

"I'm the plumber," says Reagan. "In Ireland, you have to be able to fix things yourself," she says. "I spent a year there in college—here—

I'll show you."

She takes us downstairs. Then we all step into the bathroom. Pale pink sink, grey tiled floor. Pale pink tiles on the wall, interrupted by larger tiles with—I'm not kidding—flamingoes in a lake with a sunset. It looks like something out of a movie. That girl/woman in *The Shape of Water* would go crazy over this bathroom.

"While you're waiting to be picked up, I'll teach you Plumbing Basics 101," Reagan says.

I have to tell you: having someone explain something to you in real time, letting you look at the bits and pieces from all the angles and put your hands on them, and smell them, is how you really learn something. I mean YouTube is good, but it's nothing like THIS. I can learn this way.

"The main requirement for plumbing," Reagan says, flexing her fingers and rotating her wrists, "is you have to have quite strong hands. It's hard work," she says. "You shouldn't romanticize it."

I hang my head in this beautiful pink and grey bathroom. Typical rich white kid, making really hard work seem cool and glamorous.

"And you can't do it when you get old. You can't bend and crawl around, and your hands stiffen. You need to make as much money as you can while you're young and then get out."

"What's teaching Pre-K like," I ask Peter trying to cover up my embarrassment, as Reagan warms up her elbows and shoulders.

"Well, the pay is pretty bad," he says, "but I like it; I like explaining things. And kids that age are completely curious. They want to know everything, and they aren't embarrassed to ask anything."

I remember being a kid like that once. And then for a second I think there's something I'm supposed to do.

But Plumbing!

I focus on the present.

Reagan says, "Let's take a holistic view." She pauses.

"People think of these fixtures as discrete things...." I raise my eyebrows. "Separate, distinct."

"I'm not sure I understand," I say.

"The sink is a 'fixture,'" says Reagan. "Fixture means the particular thing that the plumbing pipes run into and out of. It's 'fixed' which means it can't move, because it's bolted down into the floor or wall."

"See," she says, waving a long large arm. "You see and think to yourself, toilet, sink, shower, but in reality it's all one connected system."

"You mean all of these . . . fixtures are connected," I say.

"Almost," she says. "The fixtures that take in fresh water and push out wastewater, like the sink and the shower are on two different sets of pipes—that's what you might call a sub-system."

This is confusing.

"Don't they get mixed up? So you're gargling with yuck water from the sink or from—" I look at the toilet.

"No," Reagan laughs. "That would be completely disgusting."

Peter joins in, "The toilet is on both the water sub-system and the sewage system because the uh, toilet stuff from there needs to go someplace different. When you flush the toilet with water you get from fresh water sub-system, the stuff in the toilet goes down into a special pipe designed to take that stuff away."

"No, honey," Reagan says. "That was in the house that we rented before this—that was on a septic system."

Peter scratches his nose and thinks.

"God, you're right. I better leave the explaining to the professional!"

They laugh, and I can see they are in love with each other. The way people are. Not like in movies or on TV but like in real life.

It's sort of embarrassing to look at.

But it's also—what would you say?—Electric.

"OK, so let me correct Peter's explanation," Reagan says. "The waste water—all of it—goes into one pipe."

"And where does all that go?" I ask.

"Out to the main sanitary sewer line that runs down the street."

I realize that must be the setup we had at home in Hancock Park.

Reagan spits in the toilet, pushes the lever, and watches the water go down the hole.

Then she starts running the faucet. But first she puts the stopper down at the bottom of the sink.

"There's the fresh water subsystem working."

"OK," I say. "So there's a fresh water subsystem that brings the good water in, and there's a waste water subsystem to take my gargle water and toothpaste water out."

"Right," says Reagan. She pulls up the stopper, and the water in the sink disappears.

"There's the waste water subsystem going into gear."

"What about hot and cold water?" I say.

Reagan crouches on the floor.

"Look here," she says.

"This is a pedestal sink, so the lines are outside and easy to see."

I crouch down too and see two lines with handles behind the pedestal part of the sink.

"That's hot and that's cold," she says. "Hot water comes in from the water heater."

"Our water heater was in a little shed where the washing machine was," I say.

"Was?" says Peter softly.

"I guess it still is," I say. "It's just—our house sort of broke."

I explain about the water backing up.

"Sounds like a clog and also inadequate pressure," Reagan says. She stands up too. She goes over to a wall near the door of the bathroom.

"See, there's what's called a vent stack and vent pipes keeps the traps sealed and prevents sewer gases from backing up through the drains."

"I think there was a hole in the sewer line or in the pipe that led out to the sewer line. That's what the man with the camera said," I say.

"Wow," says Peter. "It sounds messed up."

"If I could see it," says Reagan. "I could probably tell you what's wrong. Was it an old house?"

"I think so," I say, "although I don't think it's as old as this house." We walk back upstairs into the main hallway and I look at the wood floors and the bannisters that look a lot like the house next door. And there's these cool wooden cabinets in the dining area.

"These are 1920 Craftsman houses," says Peter. "The plumbing though—that's been completely redone, hasn't it, and the electrical?"

"Yeah," says Reagan, "But I want to clarify something." She waves me over, and we walk into the kitchen.

"There can be a fixture problem too, like for example, the faucets on the sink might stop working."

"Faucets have a lot of parts," I say. "I took one apart once."

She nods.

"Also, the stuff in the toilet itself can get screwed up. Like that thing that bobs in the place behind the toilet."

"The tank?" Reagan says.

"Yeah, the tank can stop working and so the tank doesn't know it's filled and keeps on filling."

"That happens a lot."

I am telling her about how I plunged the toilets at camp and stuck coins to the bobbing thing so it would lie down flat and the tank would stop filling.

We are talking about this when the car comes.

"Nice meeting you, Sarassine," says Reagan. I can tell she wants to hug me. Adults are like that. They want to hug you all the time. But she doesn't. She shakes my hand instead.

Her handshake makes me feel good, like I was an adult too. Which, in a way, I am.

Peter shakes my hand again too.

"Here," he says. He hands me a card.

```
+---------------------------------------+
|                                       |
|                                       |
|          Reagan McCarthy              |
|            Plumbing                   |
|                                       |
|          Claremont, CA                |
|                                       |
|                                       |
+---------------------------------------+
```

"If you ever want her to come out and look at the situation."

Reagan laughs. "I'm terrible at promoting myself, so it's a good thing he does it!"

"It's kind of far for you to go, isn't it?" I say.

"Not as a professional courtesy, it isn't," Reagan says. "From one plumber to another."

I smile at that.

"OK," I say. "Thanks."

The chauffeur gets out of the car and presents her identification. For a second I thought it might the apprentice chauffeur from the day that started it all. But it isn't.

But that's OK.

I get in the car, and the chauffeur shuts the door.

The writer appears at the window. He points in the direction of the church.

OMG!

I roll down the window.

"Peter!!!!"

He comes over to the car.

"Do you know any lawyers?"

He leans over. "Why?"

"There's are two kids hiding in the garage at the church," I say. "Something to do with ... ICE, and there's another kid who—"

He puts his hand up.

"Don't say any more," he says. "We're part of a rapid response team." He pulls out his cell phone and starts talking fast as he walks away from the car.

"You coming too?" I say to the writer. Reagan is talking to the chauffeur and suggesting alternate routes to avoid the worst traffic.

Peter turns back to me briefly. Still with his phone to his ear, he nods at me, and gives me a thumbs up.

Which I think means "We'll handle it."

The writer writes, *No, I need to help Dylan with his novel* in the air.

I think of something else.

It's a bit of a stretch but I consider how in practical Kabbalah under certain circumstances it really is OK to summon the dead and I think about Dylan's mother's coats and the picture of her in the frame. I think really hard, and then I squeeze my eyes closed, and since I don't know the Yiddish, I just have to try in English, so I wave both hands in a little circle and mutter:

Come

The driver gets in the car.

"Did you need something, Miss?"

"No," I say.

I wave to Peter and Reagan. The writer nods at me and writes in the air. "*GOODBYE.*"

As we back out, I take a careful look at next door.

The house is quiet. Dark.

But I could swear I hear water running.

And on the doorstep, a woman in a tight white dress gets to her feet and hands her large white purse to the writer, who appears at her side. She puts her hand on the door knocker. They stand together waiting for the door to open.

I think, *Tell him.... something, anything that feels true.... But please don't let him be so alone.*

Then I start crying in the fancy black car, because I just turned fourteen and I fell in love with a camper and a drug dealer and I saw spirits and I made a friend who is hiding from ICE, and I finally understand a little how plumbing systems work.

All those connections that are unseen, that run under the road of things.

CHAPTER 29

So Grandpa died while I was at two dysfunctional Jewish camps in Simi Valley and was quasi-abducted and then briefly hid out with a drug dealer in Claremont and met three kids who were actual runaways, two of whom were actually running from actual cops who wanted to put them in actual concentration camps.

Hans Anfang had a stroke and he died quickly in his apartment in the kitchen with professional wrestling blaring on the TV as he sat in one of those very ugly paisley chairs. That's what Grandma tells me at the big house in Pacific Palisades, along with a rabbinical intern, and her friend, who is this tall guy who is some kind of minister.

I hear this and feel really bad about our last conversation. But then I'm so tired that I go to sleep in the little pink bedroom that I always used to sleep in when I went to visit Grandma and Grandpa long ago. Then I get up, scrounge a bagel, eat another bagel, and help myself to half a croissant from a bakery that Grandma says is "to die for" and then the chauffeur girl drives me and Grandma to what's left of my house in Hancock Park.

All that's left is some framing and I guess the foundation.

"We hadda take it down to the studs," Mr. Pasternak explains to me when I arrive on the scene.

OF COURSE he remains the constant. Of course he's still there. Apparently, he didn't go back to Jaffa and is still here even though my father hates him and from what I can see he's a pretty terrible sub-contractor.

He has a new set of men working for him, all speaking languages that are different. He seems to understand them all, and he is showing plans to another man, who is also tall but big and bearish.

Oh yes, Ryan the depressed contractor. He finally makes his appearance at the very end of this story.

My grandmother goes over and talks to him in a quiet but intense voice about something she wants him to do in HER house.

So.... the housing improvements continue, it seems.

It's hot because this is Southern California in the summer, and I am about to just sit on what's left of the grass, when I notice that there is a toilet sitting on the curb. I think it's the toilet from the guest bathroom.

I fold the lid down and sit on it.

I wait.

"Oh," says Mr. Pasternak, after he has finished talking with Ryan the depressed contractor. "This letter is for you."

He hands me an envelope,

Griselda Anfang it reads in the upper left-hand corner.

There is no stamp though.

My mom.

I open it.

July ....

Dear Sarassine—

Your dad and I are in Israel on behalf of Jews for a Two-state Solution. We didn't tell you about any of this, because we were afraid we would not be able to enter the country, because of the crack down on BDS activism or on anyone who is critical of the Israeli government these days.

We are working hard here trying to help bring people who don't agree with each other at all together. I don't know if we will succeed, but we have to try.

I am sorry for all the mystery. Mr. Pasternak has a cousin who travels between the US and Israel a lot, and she is bringing the letter by hand, and hopefully it will reach you.

I hope you are having a good summer at camp, and please know that we both love you.

Your grandmother can be difficult, but I think in her heart she is a good person.

Love always—

Mom

PS—I converted to Judaism in Jerusalem! My Hebrew name is Naomi to go with yours—Ruth. Xoxo

"I was gonna mail that to you with like FEDEX," Mr. Pasternak says. "But that crazy camp wouldn't let me send it, and then *they* had all those plumbing problems, and I guess an earthquake...." He pauses. He sits on the ruined grass next to me.

"Say," he says to me. "You know ... you got some kind of power to make what is below surface, come out!" he says.

I shrug. "I guess I'm a typical teenager. I blow things up."

He nods. Then he sits on the curb and lights a cigarette. He offers me one as he looks up at me on my displaced porcelain seat.

I decline. Those things will kill you.

"Me too. I was like that too, as a kid. But then I found that with that power you also have the opposite. You have the power to repair things, close up the gaps, make the supports stronger."

I lift my eyebrows at this. At this point Bobby the cat shows up and walks in and out and around our legs.

"And then what—" I say. "You bury that shit back down again? Literally?" I can feel myself getting mad.

He inhales deep and exhales. "*Lo,* not exactly. See—all that stuff that makes things work, all those tubes and lines and pipes, they don't wanna be seen most of the time; they wanna to do their job, and that job is better done down below. And once you see 'em you don't need to see 'em all the time to know they are there."

He stands up.

"They do their best work subterranean like, Sarassine," he says "until they need to come up, or you need to dig, explore, search to find what's wrong."

I look up at him. He is a pretty cool guy. "Hey," I say. "I don't know your first name—what is it?"

"Abed."

"That's not Hebrew is it?"

"No," says Abed Pasternak. "One of my grandmothers was Palestinian—and so is my wife."

I look up the street.

A girl is walking towards us. Quickly. She waves.

She has a short orange skirt on and bright pink Converses.

I wave back.

The girl runs and I run and we hug.

"I thought you might not recognize me," says the person who was Charlus and who then became Jackie.

"You're just the same," I say. "Only—you're different."

She laughs.

I bow and offer her the toilet on the curb. She seats herself with a flourish.

"What is your name, now?" I say.

"I decided on a name sort of like my boy name," she says. "Carlotta. Pronouns are she and her."

Carlotta tells me about the trans teen summer camp she found and the friends she made there. How her Aunt from Goshen, Indiana, who was a stripper and something of a porn personality in amateur Midwest video, came out and did an intervention on Carlotta's parents.

"And they actually listened?" I say. "Incredible."

"It can happen," says Carlotta. "*Tout est possible.*"

I am listening to Carlotta who is—I forgot to mention—wearing cool fishnets under her skirt and Converses, and I'm thinking about my adventures.

"Can we watch a movie together sometime?" I say.

"Sure," says Carlotta. I'm really interested in movies with transgender and nonbinary characters in them."

"I get that," I say. "I'm interested in that too, even though I don't think I'm trans."

As I say that I realize it's complicated. I think about Victor at the senior citizens' Jewish camp, and I remember my pretending to be a boy and how, as strong a feeling as it was, how that is very different from actually wanting to physically be a boy. I think that I'm a girl, just not a girly-girl, but not a tom boy either, but something else, and I think I may prefer boys to girls sexually but I'm not sure about that either. But the main thing is that being something else—whatever that something else is—is OK, because Carlotta will always be my friend and I will be hers. I know that.

I look up the street and see the limousine chauffeur driving a pair of people who look a lot like my parents, and as they pull into the driveway of our non-house, I feel angry as hell at them, but at the same time, relieved. Because we are a messed-up family, but you know … it's better than being a drug dealer in a deserted family house or in a garage with the cops after you, or worse, no one at all to go back to, and not even being regarded as a person at all.

My mom gets out of the car.

She stands looking at me. I look at her. We are very different, and she has a lot of explaining to do about this international traveling and in particular the trip to Israel, but I guess it will all come together. Or it won't. Either way, it's OK.

"Jesus, mom—aren't you going to hug me?" I say. I figure I'll start right in with the guilt trip.

Then she does hug me. And I hug her too.

I hug my dad next.

Carlotta sits on her toilet looking on, while my grandmother looks at me meaningfully and says, "Oh, what a time Sarassine has had with those two **fakakta** camps," (one of which she recommended) and then "*Mazel tov* on your conversion!"

And she kisses my mother.

I think about Grandpa and how lucky he was to have escaped the Nazis.

"Two summer camps?" my mother says.

"I'll explain latah," says my grandmother.

I'm not sure I want to be a plumber any more. I'd rather be a contractor. Like Ryan

How's your Yiddish?

oh come on, you can figure out this one, can't you? "**Fakakta**" means "messed up", "not working"," crappy."

only with better meds and a better therapist: the person who has plans who sees the big picture. Or an actor. Or a teacher. Or maybe I'll clean houses. Doing dishes and sweeping up—those are actually important jobs.

As if on cue, I look up the street and see Tomy and Sofia arriving at someone else's house.

"Miss," says one of the workmen to me. "Here is the plunger we found next to the bathroom, when we took it apart. In my family it's good luck to take something from the bathroom, that's the realest part of the house. Something to remember the house by—to remember it as it really was."

Grandma pulls a replacement copy of *Practical Kabbalah for Total Schlubs* out of her giant black designer bag. She is speaking quietly and quickly as Bobby the cat sits looking at her. She extends her arm to the street, as three men take shape before her. A warrior, an escape artist, and her almost ex-husband.

"So, it was you who summoned those three guys," I say to her.

"No, there are just two," she says. At that, Grandpa smiles, puts his index finger to his lips.

"To be honest, Sarassine, I felt hahrrible," Grandma says to me. "I felt hahribble that I was not always kind to your father, because he always cared more about doing the right thing than making mahney. I felt hahribble that I wasn't happier to be alive after the motorcycle accident. I felt ashamed that I wasn't grateful. But you can't summon gratitude. So that

 TA-DA! The mystery is revealed!

The escape artist turns out to be none other than Harry Houdini the famous magician whose specialty was escaping from boxes under water all chained up and/ or handcuffed. He really WAS the son of a rabbi, which I personally find hilarious, and he also seemed to have believed in spirits himself, so he must feel vindicated that he can be one. He also wrote about and explained magic tricks because he didn't want people to be fooled, which is very interesting and kind of rabbinic of him, imho. See https://en.wikipedia.org/wiki/Harry_Houdini

made me feel guilty. And the guilt made me feel angry. So—I admit it—I overreacted a little to you and your friend at the house. And then you got lost, and I knew it was at least partly my fault and not just your perrents' and your grandfather's. We are living in a time without role models, so I summoned a couple, based on some his-tahrical mystery novels I've been reading by a very gifted Flahrida author. They weren't the ideal ones perhaps, but they were the ones that came. And sometimes you just have to take what you can get, do you know what I am saying?"

"I told you," says Carlotta. "*Une sorcière.*"

Grandma shrugs her shoulders and leans against a quite good-looking black Mercedes, which is not hers, goes into her bag, and pulls out a box of Godiva chocolates. She holds the box out to me and Carlotta.

We each take a chocolate.

"Nice spirits," says my dad. "Isn't that Houdini with all the chains?"

"Such a nice boy," says my grandmother. "And so successful!"

The six of them begin to chant the *shehecheyanu*, the Hebrew blessing that has brought us to this moment.

I'm wondering why only I can see my grandpa. I guess spirits can read minds because he stops reciting the prayer and materializes right next to me.

"I came for you," he says. "Please forgive me for disappointing you at the end."

"I forgive you," I say. I feel myself getting ready to cry.

"Well, it's about time," says Grandma to me. "And OF COURSE I forgive **you**, Sarassine, for all the trahble you caused earlier this summer."

Can a spirit laugh? Grandpa's spirit holds his astral stomach and shakes, or perhaps it's just him disappearing. Which he does.

An Orthodox family walks by our group on the street. The parents stop to greet my mother, father, and grandmother.

While Mr. Pasternak engages the group in a lively discussion about house reconstruction in a combination of English, Hebrew, and Yiddish, three small kids come over to us.

"Welcome back home!" one tiny girl says to me. She has that beautiful high voice that some little kids have.

I look past her to the fading form of Shimon Bar Kokhba. He nods at me, and points to his ear.

God's small voice. Listen.

I hold the plunger and talk with my friend. Carlotta takes things out of my good old backpack: Grandma's book; the orange and green threads from Grandpa's kitchen chairs; the mezuzah from Camp Baruch Bardot; the little battery from the box used in summoning Jewish Historical Figures (who, as it turns out, I didn't summon after all); my claim-ticket for the Claremont shoe repair; Estrella's bead necklace with the cross on it (that Carlotta tells me is called a "rosary"); and Reagan's business card.

I tell her the stories connected to each thing. I tell her what I've learned about pressure, about effort, about repetition, about turning and twisting and fixing faucets. I tell her that getting water is a complicated process of connection, relying on systems and relationships that cross all matter of borders; water flowing in and the waste flowing out—down to the river, and out to the sea. And of that water coming back to us, clean, flowing from the taps, and us lifting a cup to our lips, and getting ready, at last, to drink.

THE END

Acknowledgments

This novel started out as a pretense, suggested by my Whidbey Writers Workshop buddy Janet Buttenwieser, when I told her that I hated pitching and didn't want to subject an actual novel manuscript to a thirty second elevator reduction. I composed the fake pitch and just for fun, started messing around with the fake novel.

This is what happens when you tell a writer to just make something up.

I began writing the voice of Sarassine Anfang, whose last name means "beginning" in German. A first draft (composed during Nanowrimo) featured a number of point of view characters. They fell away, but Sarassine held, and she would not let me go until I had told her story. I loved writing every word of this book.

I told wonderful nature artist Ann Brantingham that I'd written a crazy novel; she read an early draft of *Pretend Plumber* and loved it, but suggested that Sarassine add parenthetical explanations for the Jewish terms. Brilliant nonfiction author Jo Scott-Coe wondered if I should submit the manuscript to Inlandia Books, and thanks to the support and encouragement of Cati Porter, artistic director, Inlandia became my press. Poet and librettist Neil Aitken worked with me intensively on two revisions, based on the helpful comments of the Inlandia editorial board. I want to thank Cati for her thoughtful content editing. Thanks to Maria Fernanda Vidaurrazaga for her copy-editing assistance. Musician, writer, and book designing maestro Mark Givens designed this beautiful book.

SoCal is a wild and wooly set of disparate spots and neighborhoods. Countless friends and family members helped me appreciate those places and here are just a few of them: the late Jackson Alberts, Kathleen Alcalá, Gloria Aviles, Kerry Bar-Cohn, Jeffrey Batchelor, John Brantingham, the late Celena Bumpus, Dennis Callaci, Mary Camarillo, Kate Flannery, the Flores Family, Tod Goldberg, liz gonzalez, Ken Johnson, Ruthie Marlenée, Pat Morton, Robert Murphy, the late Elizabeth Newstat, Ruth Nolan, Mary Anne Perez, Tiffany Poremba, Lynn and Mark Rogo, Jennifer Separazadeh and the Separzadeh family, the late Theda Shapiro, and Vickie Vértiz.

Justin Scott Coe contributed valuable information about water systems in Southern California cities.

Some historical, architectural, and geographical details pertaining to the Anfangs are drawn from my memories of my generous in-laws, the late Peter and Charlotte Behrendt. I thank them for being a wonderful second set of parents, and I thank my siblings in-law, David Bar-Cohn, Judy Behrendt, and Leah Kops for sharing their family with me with unfailing largesse and kindness. Some of the behaviors of Hans Anfang and his wife are inspired by my own parents, the late Leonard and Barbé Hammer, who really should have been Jewish. I miss them both enormously and remember them with love. I thank my mother for her love of German and her devotion to mystery novels, and I thank my father for his tallness, his fast metabolism, his humility, and his ability to know how and when to apologize.

Genius at large and the most interesting person I know, Lillian Behrendt (my spawn), shared notable bat mitzvah experiences as well as an extensive knowledge of professional wrestling.

I am fortunate to know and have learned from many inspiring rabbis: Jonathan Aaron, Arik Ascherman, Sara Bassin, the late Rachel Cowan, Stephen Einstein, Mimi Feigelson, Laura Geller, Lisa Goldstein, Yohanna Kinberg, Idit Lev, and Jill Zimmerman have said or written things about Judaism that somehow played into this story. That said, the errors in Jewish learning, history and theology are all Sarassine's, as are all mistakes with Hebrew. In other words, mine.

A special thank you to the members of the HINENI community, an online congregation without walls that spans affiliations and nations. And another to author Anthony Le Donne, who writes—poignantly—about his experience of God's silence.

There is, to date, no medication for dyspraxia. Errors in description of the syndrome are all mine.

Thank you to *Wikipedia* for offering open source starting points for every possible area of knowledge in 321 different languages. A list of specific pages consulted follows.

I wrote *Pretend Plumber* far away from Southern California in the verdant and cloudy Pacific Northwest. Whidbey Island neighbor Susan Waters and Whidbey Writing Workshop alumna, novelist Deborah Nedelman always asked me what I was writing. Hilary Henry Neff sent unending support from down the road in Useless Bay. Poets Daniel Edward Moore and Laura L. Coe have created a beautiful community in the Oak Harbor Poetry Project, and I am grateful for their welcoming support. Freeland friend Babette Thompson always makes me feel like what I am writing is important. And a big thank you to Meg Olson over at the Kingfisher Bookstore in Coupeville for reserving a prominent space for us local writers.

I lived and worked in Southern California for 30 years, and I am grateful more than I can say to the students, faculty, and staff at the University of California, Riverside, who first made me aware of the plight of undocumented workers, students, and families in California and beyond. I am also thankful to the Teachers Against Child Detention, the activists of WAISN (Washington Immigration Solidarity Network), and the activists and elected officials that I met in El Paso, Texas in 2019 for heightening my awareness of US detention and deportation practices.

Green Olive Tours and ICAHD (Israeli Committee Against House Demolitions) bring visitors to the West Bank and to neighborhoods in East Jerusalem; my conversations with these organizers, as well as with visitors to and the personnel at the American Colony Hotel in East Jerusalem in 2019 helped me understand a bit more about the inequities happening in Jerusalem and elsewhere in Israel and Palestine. I send my respect and appreciation to Rabbis for Human Rights, Combatants for Peace, and all those doing the hardest work of all: the work of equity and peace in a place where justice feels both out of reach and absolutely necessary. I want to also express my admiration and love for my family in Israel, who daily navigate this difficult, transformative challenge.

I write about LGBTQIA people because some of the bravest, most brilliant individuals I know happen to belong in this category. I wish to acknowledge in particular these writer-activist-artists: Ryka Aoki, Linda Besemer, Jill Davidson, Max Delsohn, the late Jocelyne Grey, Robert Gross, Marie Hartung, Noel Pablo Mariano, Wryly Tender McCutchen, Montserrat Padilla, Amy Spalding, Erika Suderburg, and Andrew Turner.

No SoCal novel acknowledgment is complete without an acknowledgment of one's therapist. Thank you, Gordon Berger (double Ph.D.), for putting up with me all these years.

A-list literary impresario and Director of Writers Bloc Presents, Andrea Grossman is everywhere in this book. Through her I've met and continue to meet everyone worth knowing in Los Angeles. Thank you for supporting my writing and for feeding me French fries.

As always, I could not have completed this book without my spouse Larry Behrendt, author and activist, who makes every place home, and who keeps on encouraging me to write fiction that—if it's going to be *this* weird—is clear and accessible. Thanks for sticking with me and thanks for always believing in me.

Thank you, dear readers, for being here and for welcoming Sarassine Anfang into your heart.

One more thank you. As I was putting the finishing touches on this work of fiction, I learned a little about a righteous Gentile by the name of Irena Sendler (or Sendlerowa), who was an actual pretend plumber. Irena walked into the Warsaw Ghetto on a regular basis, and carried out Jewish children hidden in baskets, bags, and toolboxes. According to one source (Hefner Plumbing [https://www.hefnerplumbing.com/the-story-of-the-lady-plumber/]), she used a false bottomed plumber's box. Irena survived the war and was nominated for the Nobel Prize. Thank you, Irena, for saving at least 2500 children. To learn more, visit: https://www.theguardian.com/world/2007/mar/15/secondworldwar.poland

Sources, Further Reading, and Discussion Questions

Because she is a young teen, Sarassine goes—as kids do—directly to *Wikipedia*. These peer-reviewed pages are in continual stages of revision, but I have done my best to provide the dates of her/my access to them.

Wikipedia Webpages Sarassine refers to

"Abracadabra." *Wikipedia.* https://en.wikipedia.org/wiki/Abracadabra. Accessed July 12, 2021.

"Aliyah." *Wikipedia.* https://en.wikipedia.org/wiki/Aliyah. Accessed July 12, 2021.

"Ashkenazi Jews." *Wikipedia.* https://en.wikipedia.org/wiki/Ashkenazi Jews. Accessed July 4, 2021.

"Collaborationism." *Wikipedia.* https://en.wikipedia.org/wiki/Collaborationism. Accessed July 4th, 2021.

"Harry Houdini." *Wikipedia.* https://en.wikipedia.org/wiki/Harry Houdini. Accessed July 12, 2021.

"Hatikvah." *Wikipedia.* https://en.wikipedia.org/wiki/Hatikvah. Accessed July 4, 2021.

"The Holocaust." *Wikipedia.* https://en.wikipedia.org/wiki/The Holocaust. Accessed July 4, 2021. Also cited is the United States Holocaust Museum archived Killing Centers overview page: https://web.archive.org/web/20170914220116/https://www.ushmm.org/wlc/en/article.php?ModuleId=10005145. Accessed July 4th, 2021.

"IDF." *Wikipedia.* https://en.wikipedia.org/wiki/Israel_Defense_ Forces. Accessed July 4, 2021.

"Kashrut." *Wikipedia.* https://en.wikipedia.org/wiki/Kashrut. Accessed July 4, 2021.

"Kibbutz." *Wikipedia.* https://en.wikipedia.org/wiki/Kibbutz. Accessed July 4, 2021.

"Labeled Diagram of the Sefirot without colors" by Thomazzo. *Wikipedia.* https://commons.wikimedia.org/wiki/ File:Sefiroticky_strom.jpg. Accessed July 12, 2021.

"Minyan." *Wikipedia.* https://en.wikipedia.org/wiki/Minyan. Accessed July 12, 2021.

"Practical Kabbalah." *Wikipedia.* (https://en.wikipedia.org/wiki/ Practical_Kabbalah. Accessed July 4, 2021.

"Rabbi Akiva." *Wikipedia.* https://en.wikipedia.org/wiki/Rabbi_ Akiva. Accessed July 12, 2021.

"Schmuck." *Wikipedia.* https://en.wikipedia.org/wiki/Schmuck_(pejorative). Accessed July 4, 2021.

"Sefirot." *Wikipedia.* https://en.wikipedia.org/wiki/Sefirot. Accessed July 12, 2021.

"Sephardi Jews." *Wikipedia.* https://en.wikipedia.org/wiki/Sephardi_Jews. Accessed July 4, 2021.

"Shema Yisrael." *Wikipedia.* See https://en.wikipedia.org/wiki/ Shema_Yisrael. Accessed July 12, 2021. See also "My Jewish Learning," https://www.myjewishlearning.com/article/the-shema/, accessed on July 12, 2021.

"Simon Bar Kokhba." *Wikipedia.* https://en.wikipedia.org/wiki/Simon_ bar_Kokhba. Accessed July 12, 2021.

"Spanish Civil War." *Wikipedia.* https://en.wikipedia.org/wiki/ Spanish_Civil_War. Accessed July 4, 2021.

"Unlabeled diagram of the Qabalistic Tree of Life," by Alan James Garner. Creative Commons Attribution-Share Alike 4.0 International license https://commons.wikimedia.org/wiki/File:Qabalistic_Tree_of_Life_Unlabelled.png. Accessed July 12, 2021.

"Yahrzeit Candle." *Wikipedia.* https://en.wikipedia.org/wiki/Yahrzeit_candle. Accessed July 12, 2021.

"Yom Kippur." *Wikipedia.* https://en.wikipedia.org/wiki/Yom_Kippur. Accessed July 4, 2021.

Perhaps you would like to know more about Judaism and the other topics mentioned in this book. Here are a few titles to get you started.

The Complete Idiot's Guide to Learning Yiddish. Rabbi Benjamin Blech. Alpha, 2000.

The Complete Idiot's Guide to Middle East Conflict. Mitchell Geoffrey Bard. Alpha, 1999.

Deported: Immigrant Policing, Disposable Labor and Global Capitalism. Tanya Maria Golash-Boza. NYU Press, 2015.

The Distance Between Us: A Memoir. Reyna Grande. Washington Square, 2013.

Encyclopedia of Occultism. Lewis Spence. Dover, 2003.

Essential Judaism: Updated. George Robinson. Atria, 2016.

The Five Books of Moses. Trans. Everett Fox. Schocken, 2000.

Girl Undercover: Growing up Transgender. Jill Davidson. Smashwords, 2012.

How to Be an Anti-Racist. Ibram X. Kendi. One World, 2019.

How to They/Them. Stuart Getty (illus. Brooke Thyng). Sasquatch, 2020.

In Search of Fatima: A Palestinian Story. Ghada Karmi. Verso, 2004.

Kabbalah for Dummies. Arthur Kurzweil. For Dummies, 2006.

The Life and Afterlife of Harry Houdini. Joe Posnanski. Avid Reader, 2019

The Middle East for Dummies. Craig S. Davis. For Dummies, 2003.

My Promised Land: The Triumph and Tragedy of Israel. Ari Shavit. Random House, 2015.

Queer, 2nd edition: the Ultimate LGBTQ Guide for Teens. Kathy Belge and Marke Bieschke. Zest Books, 2019.

The Rise and Fall of the Third Reich: A History of Nazi Germany. William Shirer. Simon and Schuster, 2011.

The Routledge History of the Holocaust. Jonathan Friedman, ed. Routledge, 2012.

Tanakh: The Holy Scriptures. Jewish Publication Society, 1985.

Discussion questions

- What kind of portrait of Los Angeles does Sarassine provide readers at the beginning of the novel? What other films and books does this picture remind you of? How is it different?

- In what ways is Sarassine a typical only child? In what ways is she atypical?

- What surprises you about Sarassine's friendship with Jackie? When Jackie calls Sarassine their "father," what does that mean and how does it change the relationship?

- There are a number of popular culture references in the beginning of the novel. What are they and how do they contribute to the atmosphere and tone of Sarassine's world?

- Why do you think Sarassine's grandfather turns her over to the Bardot Camp counselors? Do you blame him? Is there a rationale for what he does that you can accept? What seems to be going on in the relationship between the grandparents?

- What are your feelings about Sarassine pretending to be genderqueer? What happens to her psychologically in the process? Discuss her romance with Hannah. How does that experience fit in with this feigned identity?

- Would you like to visit or—if you are older—live at the Ahava Retirement Center? Why or why not?

- Judaism and Jewish identity play a big role, both in Sarassine's view of her world and in the way she tells her story. How might this novel read if it were told by a Christian, Muslim, or Buddhist narrator? And how does Sarassine's view of herself as a Jewish person evolve?

- What is the attitude on the part of the seniors towards the question of Israel and Palestine? In what ways is this at odds with their attempted secret ritual? Or is it at odds?

- Discuss Sarassine's relationship with Dylan. What's good about it? What's dangerous about it?

- How is Sarassine changed through her encounters with Estrella and Peter? What does she learn about herself?

About the Author

Stephanie Barbé Hammer is a 7-time Pushcart Prize nominee in fiction, nonfiction and poetry. She has published in the *Bellevue Literary Review, Hayden's Ferry Review,* and *Café Irreal*. She is the author of the poetry collections *Sex with Buildings* and *How Formal?* as well as a novel, *The Puppet Turners of Narrow Interior*, and a novelette, *Rescue Plan*.

Originally from Manhattan, Stephanie lived in Southern California for 30 years and now currently resides on Whidbey Island, Washington State.

www.stephaniebarbehammer.net

About Inlandia Institute

Inlandia Institute is a regional literary non-profit and publishing house. We seek to bring focus to the richness of the literary enterprise that has existed in this region for ages. The mission of the Inlandia Institute is to recognize, support, and expand literary activity in all of its forms in Inland Southern California by publishing books and sponsoring programs that deepen people's awareness, understanding, and appreciation of this unique, complex and creatively vibrant region.

The Institute publishes books, presents free public literary and cultural programming, provides in-school and after school enrichment programs for children and youth, holds free creative writing workshops for teens and adults, and boot camp intensives. In addition, every two years, the Inlandia Institute appoints a distinguished jury panel from outside of the region to name an Inlandia Literary Laureate who serves as an ambassador for the Inlandia Institute, promoting literature, creative literacy, and community. Laureates to date include Susan Straight (2010–2012), Gayle Brandeis (2012–2014), Juan Delgado (2014–2016), Nikia Chaney (2016–2018), and Rachelle Cruz (2018–2020).

To learn more about the Inlandia Institute, please visit our website at www.InlandiaInstitute.org.

Inlandia Books

ladybug by Nikia Chaney

More Dreamers of the Golden Dream by Susan Straight, Douglas Mc-Culloh, and Delphine Sims

Güero-Güero: The White Mexican and Other Published and Unpublished Stories by Dr. Eliud Martínez

A Short Guide to Finding Your First Home in the United States: An Inlandia anthology on the immigrant experience

Care: Stories by Christopher Records

San Bernardino, Singing, edited by Nikia Chaney

Facing Fire: Art, Wildfire, and the End of Nature in the New West by Douglas McCulloh

Writing from Inlandia, an annual anthology (2011–)

In the Sunshine of Neglect: Defining Photographs and Radical Experiments in Inland Southern California, 1950 to the Present by Douglas McCulloh

Henry L. A. Jekel: Architect of Eastern Skyscrapers and the California Style by Dr. Vincent Moses and Catherine Whitmore

Orangelandia: The Literature of Inland Citrus edited by Gayle Brandeis

While We're Here We Should Sing by The Why Nots

Go to the Living by Micah Chatterton

No Easy Way: Integrating Riverside Schools - A Victory for Community by Arthur L. Littleworth

9 781955 969048